Also by K Iwancio

The Gift Across the Street

Bed...& Breakfast

Breakfast in Bed

Spellbound in the Stacks

Behind the Pages

Enjoy the
Romancing the Pages
playlist!

Romancing the Pages

K. Iwancio

This is a work of fiction. The characters, organizations, and events portrayed in this novel are either products of the author's imagination, have been granted permission to use, or are used factiously. References to public figures, celebrities, and fictional characters outside my fandom are used with the utmost compliments.

Romancing the Pages. Copyright ©2023 by K. Iwancio.

2nd Edition. 2024.

All rights reserved. Printed in the United States of America.

Chapter One

"Sex sells, Mari. That's the truth. That's where the market is at right now." Reminded Faith Wild, Mari Quay's literary agent. With a name like 'Faith Wild', and her vivid imagination, she could have been a bestselling author. But Faith didn't want to bother. She was content to push talented authors' works to print rather than write herself. "Besides, I've seen your social media. Your fans want more spice in your books!"

Mari groaned into the phone as her hand ran down her face in her exasperation. Faith was right. But Mari could still hate every part of the truth. The readers on her social media continued to speak in droves, all demanding the same thing.

More sex.

More romance.

More love.

Mari was Write Type Publishing's newest and most consistent bestselling author. She was currently on trend to produce 1-2 new novels yearly. The fans were gobbling them up as fast as the company could print them. Both of her books in the last few years eventually made it to number one on the bestsellers list. A feat that new authors rarely ever got to see.

Faith wanted Mari to continue her upward trend and ride that wave to the bank. Once an author met their stride, it was imperative to at least attempt to keep up with it. Or at least tease their fans and leave them begging for more. But right now, Mari didn't even have an idea to pitch.

"I know…I know… I've read…most of the comments." Mari released a heady sigh. The anxiety bubbled up deep inside her gut. She loved writing and was ecstatic that she could write as her full-time job now. Except for the fact that her fans and publisher's demands were taking the wind out of her creative sales. "I'm not gonna lie. It's honestly freaking me out."

"What? Why? You've written a little bit of almost everything. Adding more spice to your next book shouldn't be difficult. Right?"

If only it were that easy.

"I mean…sure?"

"Come on, Mari. I know you can do this." There was a prolonged silence that bordered on uncomfortable. "Look, I hate repeating myself. But the publisher is getting impatient waiting for your new book. You have to give them an idea soon or… You could be looking for a new one."

"I know. I know." This was the third phone call in a month from Faith. Time was ticking down at an alarming rate, and she needed to think of something. Would it be so awful if she took the time, time that she was running out of, to research and write a more romance-centric novel?

The short answer?
Yes.
The long answer?
Also, yes.

She had to give the people what they were asking for. No matter what she had to do to get there. Including all the awkwardness of attempting something new and unknown to her.

"Okay. Fine. Tell them it's a dramatic contemporary romance and that I'm working on the details. Could be YA. Or maybe it will stay in adult fiction. I'm still…tinkering with things."

The audible squeal was sharp. Mari needed to move the phone away from her ear as Faith released her excitement in one elongated breath. At least now she could placate the poor woman and buy herself some much-needed time. The genre and theme were already well in hand. Now all she needed was the story.

"Oh, you just made this agent one happy woman! I'm going to email them immediately. You know they'll want a synopsis ASAP so…chop, chop!"

"Yes, yes. I'm on it." Mari dismissed the bubbly nature that permeated through the phone. Her voice had gone strained with her oncoming stress. "I'm going to at least attempt to get something written up today. But I should have some smattering of something by the end of the week."

"That's my girl! Okay, I'll leave you to it!"

Mari clicked the 'end call' button and dropped her phone onto her antique desk with a jarring thud. In utter silence she sat and stared at her keyboard, feeling lost. Dropping her forehead to the desk's surface, she let out a shrill shriek.

What the fuck was she going to do?

Of course, she was being overdramatic. She was Mari Quay. A bestselling author with her young adult fantasy and adult fiction books. She had her hands in two different genres and two different audiences. And yet the cry was always the same:

Give us more!

She had an undeniable knack for creating and developing complex characters and relationships. The dialogue she provided gave the characters such a realistic quality. Almost as if you were reading it while watching a notable actor's performance. There was palpable tension between the characters. Her words made them jump off the page. So much so that the audience could see the chemistry that pulled them together. With little tangible and tantalizing teases here and there.

She could never bring it upon herself to let her characters go further than a basic attraction. That was for one reason, and one reason only.

Mari had never been in love.

Sure, there were quick flings and one-night stands here and there. But she had never been in a relationship for longer than a few months. Nothing long enough to get a proper gauge of feelings. Especially for anything beyond the initial physical attraction and nowhere near enough experience to write about it and make it believable.

It's not that she wasn't attractive. Well, attractive may be a stretch, but she wasn't unfortunate looking. Mari had the "girl next door" vibe down to an effortless science. Effortless was how she liked to keep it. She was a no-makeup, t-shirt and jeans kind of girl, her hair was always up in a ponytail. Her look was topped off with gold-rimmed glasses from years of reading with questionable light sources.

With her glasses, darkened blonde hair, and blue-green eyes, she turned a head or two. Not that she would have ever noticed such a thing. She was oblivious to even the most obvious advances. That is, if she ever put herself in a situation to receive such attention.

She was a borderline recluse. Ever since the pandemic, she had been happy spending most of her days at home. It had been her mental saving grace. While others were home and freaking out, Mari spent time writing and enjoying the quiet. In the last year, she had been able to quit her job to write full-time. She was living her best life. Finally.

Mari enjoyed her peace. Even more so now with the new townhouse. She had built it with her first bestselling book advance and royalties. It backed up to a wooded area with a quaint, meandering stream and she was content to live a more laid-back life. Sometimes the three-bedroom townhouse felt a bit much for her. But with the space, she was able to have the office/library of her dreams.

Sometimes she wondered what finding that special "someone" would be like. Someone to share her home and life with. To celebrate her victories and encourage her despite her failures. To have someone beside her in bed when she felt those heated urges. As those fleeting thoughts appeared, they would evaporate back to nothing.

The single life had been kind to her for the most part. Her friends on social media posted daily about relationship and family stressors. It was an endless stream of kids, work, partner woes, divorce, and the horrors of the dating world. All Mari needed were a handful of posts with that nonsense and she was quite happy again with her life choices. Who would be willing to sign up for all that extra stress? All because of love? No thanks.

Although having some sort of semblance of a family would be nice. Her parents passed away within a few years of each other after she had graduated college. Being an only child, with no extended family left, she had no one to check in with or report her ongoings. It had made holidays rather difficult to go through alone. Through the years, she had managed to set her own traditions. Or give in to her friends' pleadings to join them in their festivities.

Right now, she was beginning to fall back into that craving to have someone. At least someone she could vent to or bounce ideas off of. When she was desperate, she talked to herself. But right now, she felt silly doing that. She had no shortage of ideas, but no one understood how her creative mind ticked. Sometimes she had managed to corner a friend to brainstorm with. But it was the middle of the workday, and they were all busy with their lives. A boyfriend or a husband would be handy about now. To be a sounding board to help her narrow down her chaotic brain.

They do that kind of shit, right?

Right?

Chapter Two

Mari sat at her keyboard with a huff. The cursor on her screen was mocking her. It flickered in a consistent pattern to match her anxious heartbeat. Nothing was coming to her. No words, no ideas, nothing. Her mind went in circles as it wandered through the quiet depths. She was accomplishing very little.

The hour had already dipped past dinner time. It was a chore to keep her eyes open, let alone sit upright at her desk and try to think of legible words. There was no point in continuing. She had to give up for the night. Falling asleep at her desk would not add to her word count. As if on cue, her stomach growled with displeasure at its empty status.

She rose from her desk with a sigh and dragged herself downstairs to find something to eat. At least she had accomplished getting dressed that day, but that had been the only thing that she managed to do. Her writer's block was proving to be extra difficult while under pressure.

Opening the refrigerator door, Mari leaned in to observe her options. There wasn't much to choose from as she had neglected to do her online grocery shopping that week. With a defeated sigh, she settled on an omelet. Might as well use up the scraps of leftovers in the best way possible. Letting the butter melt into the warming pan, she stared at it in deep thought. Or was it more of a mindless spacing?

Grabbing an egg, she cracked it into the pan along with two others before tossing the shells into the sink. Cooking was methodical, a good escape for the mind. There was a routine to it, a somewhat cemented chain of events that needed to be completed before the end result. It was almost like writing a story. Each step always differed from the last. In the end, you had a meal waiting for you.

Writing followed roughly the same equation. You acquired a finished result but with a different narrative each time. Mari rarely abandoned any of her projects over the last few years. Did they all get published? No. But at least they were all completed works. Or well, would be. Eventually. Maybe.

Her lagoon water gaze was transfixed on the eggs in the pan. There was something poetic about breaking something. Having its contents pour out only for it to transform into something new and delicious with a little bit of heat. That was when Mari felt that familiar flutter in her heart.

She finally had an idea.

Well, more of a general direction for her next book. She added the bits and pieces of mushrooms and chopped peppers as her mind contemplated what do to next. She needed to add romance. Okay, a female lead with a male love interest. Obvious enough.

Mari liked to be unique with her written works. She knew all the troupes and whatnot, but she only ever wanted to be chasing something new. Something different.

Mari needed to write this down immediately.

The words were starting to tumble out and she had nothing to jot her ideas down onto. She hated writing notes on paper as they were always vague and unforgiving. Ideas had to be fleshed out while the iron was hot. Especially after such a long dry spell.

Dumping the contents of the pan onto a plate, she made sure to turn off the burner. Pouring herself a drink, she shoved a fork into her pile of eggs. Juggling the contents in her arms, she carried her dinner up the stairs back to her office. With a clatter, she placed her plate and glass down on her desk. Plopping down into her desk chair, she immediately began typing.

Her eggs had become lukewarm in the time she had written down her brief synopsis. Leaning back in her chair, she took a moment to clear her jumble of thoughts. She cut up her omelet with her fork as her eyes flitted about the screen to reread what she had written. It wasn't her best synopsis, but it was decent enough to send to Faith. Maybe it would even placate the publisher while Mari settled on a game plan to complete this project.

As she settled back in her desk chair to take a well-deserved brain break, her phone buzzed with a phone call. Groaning, Mari glanced down as her hand hovered over the 'ignore' button. She was ready to dismiss whoever had disturbed her. The only thing that made her hesitate was seeing the name of her best friend, Shannon Kohler-Walker. It flashed up on her screen along with a rather comical photo of the two from last summer.

As much as she despised talking on the phone, it had been some time since she had talked to Shannon. Despite the break in her writer's block, she knew she was creatively maxed out for the day. It wasn't like her writing was going anywhere fast. She answered the call.

"Hey!"

"Hey, girl! Congrats on the success of your last book! I can't believe it's still on the bestseller list six months later. That's insane. Like, you're legit a magician or something."

Mari couldn't help but chuckle at her friend. Shannon never beat around the bush when it came to their conversations. She said things that came into her brain without filtering them first. Most of the time they were amusing but other times it was something that took Mari by surprise. All in good humor at least.

"I can't believe it myself most days. Especially now that I can stay home and write all the time. Although it's not all it's cracked up to be. Faith and the publisher are beating down my door for a new book."

"Fuck that noise. Why can't they just sit back and let you write? You know what the hell you're doing."

Laughing outright, Mari nodded even though Shannon couldn't see her through the phone. Those outside of the publishing world had no idea how complex, demanding, and downright exhausting it was behind the scenes. It wasn't only about writing. There was editing, social media, marketing, appeasing too many heads, and sedating rabid fans. It was not for the faint of heart.

"One would think. I wish the industry was that easy. But it's not. It's like every other one. Always worried about the almighty dollar." Mari grew more restless as she rambled on. "Why do these publishers need to censor the artist? Just let us work and stop micromanaging for fucks sake."

Shannon made a rumbling noise of approval. "You tell them bitches!"

"I wish. I got berated today about taking so long to figure out a new project. It either needs to appease the publisher or else they'll drop you. And then you have to go through all the bullshit to placate another one. I don't have the brainpower to bother with that."

"Sooooo…do you have a new idea or not?"

"Well…sort of."

"Sort of? What the hell does that mean?"

"It means I'm fucked. Unless I can make this fragile idea stick or go back to the drawing board and think of something else. But right now, I'm just…stuck."

"Mari has writer's block? Shit. The world is coming to an end. Or maybe I should play the lottery."

"Oh, fuck you."

"Language!" Shannon teased with a chuckle. Meanwhile, she had already dropped her share of expletives a handful of times in their short conversation.

"Yeah, yeah. It's beginning to affect my livelihood at this point. I could be going stir-crazy. I can't remember the last time I left my house for a measurable amount of time. I'm becoming a crazy ol' hermit, bunkered down from the rest of the world."

"Yeah. You are." Shannon immediately agreed. "You can't even manage to spare an afternoon with your bestie and pretend you're human. You need at least that sometimes." There was a prolonged silence between both of the women. "That's it! I have a fucking brilliant as fuck idea for fucks sake."

"Language." Mari reminded Shannon with a burst of laughter.

"Why don't you come down to the beach? You know…for the summer."

"Shannon, I already do that. Every year you ask when I'm going to come to stay-"

"No, I mean the *whole* summer! Look, I know Luke won't be super thrilled with the idea of giving up the rental income above the bakery. But we are going to need to hire a few more people anyway. You'd just be…built-in help."

"Wait, are you volun-telling me that I can spend the entire summer at the beach as long as I work it off?"

"Basically? Yeah. You can stay at the beach for the whole summer without the crushing and awful guilt you'd have from stealing." Mari laughed out loud at Shannon's suggestion. It wasn't a terrible idea. "Change of scenery. Meet new people. Get your hands dirty for once… It could fuel a whole shit-ton of fodder for your writing. Plus, then we can actually hang out the whole summer instead of you sneaking off for a random week. What do you say?"

Shannon wasn't wrong. It was too good of an idea to pass up. The beach, well, moving water for that matter, always did wonders for Mari's psyche. Not to mention that the shore was an endless supply of inspiration and calming vibes. She always wrote her best when she was in view of the water. Especially with the beloved sweet breezes off of the Atlantic.

"Are you sure?"

"Yes, I'm fucking sure. My best friend needs to get her mojo back more than we need to rent out the apartment to a zillion frat boys at once."

Inhaling through clenched teeth, Mari contemplated the offer one last time. The bakery was open from 8 am until 2 pm with prep work beginning at 4 am. They wouldn't be the most ideal conditions to work with, but she would still have a good chunk of the day to write. Even if Shannon gave her a full 40-hour week of work to keep up with the popularity of the bakery.

"Okay. Fuck it. Fine. I'll do it. But I'm not responsible for any baking fuck ups on my account."

There was a squawk of resounding laughter through the phone. "Oh my god, Mari. I've seen you bake. You aren't allowed anywhere near anything until it's good and baked. I don't have that good of an insurance policy."

"Smart choice. So, what…when would you need me?"

"Well…if you want to come around mid-May, the week before Memorial Day, that would be fucking fantastic. Like…by the Friday before at the very latest. But the apartment is free. Just show up at my house, like the stalker that you are, and I'll give you the key."

There was a prolonged silence between the two friends. Mari considered how her summer was going to go from that point on.

"Thanks, Shannon. I think this will be just the thing I need."

Chapter Three

Mari stood on the balcony of the apartment over the bakery and breathed in with delight. Her nostrils tinged with the sharp tang of the soothing sea air. It was salty with a tinge of the faintest scent of fish from the bay that was a few blocks to the west. The thin strip of land dubbed the "Seven Mile Isle" stood between the best of both worlds, the bay and the Atlantic Ocean. It was close and yet still far enough from the mainland of New Jersey to enjoy the lax lifestyle of a classy beach town.

Avalon, New Jersey lived up to its namesake of a magical island in the tale of King Arthur. The fabled king had used it as a place to escape after he was wounded in battle. Most vacationed there as a week-long getaway or second home away from the hustle and bustle of the city life of Philadelphia and New York.

Although no castle resided there, it was still majestic in its own right. Homes were colorful and lovely, all sorted out into neat rows down short streets. The town itself was charming. With lively shops, chic restaurants, and eateries, it was a draw for families up and down the East Coast. It had a quiet and easy-going charm that Mari had grown to love. The town had a special place in her heart ever since Shannon had first invited her to stay there during the summer.

A few years ago, Shannon had moved back to the shore to take on her family's business. Her parents had grown too elderly to deal with the usual rigors of running a popular bakery. So, she stepped in to help.

As a pet project after their early retirement, Shannon's parents purchased the bakery. They had turned it into a staple of the local community. With word of mouth, it had become a must-visit destination. Most returning vacationing families made it a tradition to stop by every year. The bakery gave the Kohlers the excuse to live down by the shore that they had fallen in love with over the decades. Shannon had always complained about the stress of owning the bakery, but her parents loved it anyway. So, when they asked Shannon to be a part of the next generation, it surprised Mari that she jumped at the chance.

Not that Mari minded. The Kohler's Bakery was the highlight of Seven Mile Isle. Families came from states away to partake in their yearly feast of Kohler's famous cream-filled donuts. Two local eateries even featured their donuts as an ice cream flavor and a breakfast pancake. They did live up to the hype. As much as she enjoyed them, it was going to be a death wish to her waistline being around them on a daily basis.

It would be a new experience for Mari to work in the food industry. She had never attempted such a fate. She could manage the front-end customer service stuff without issue. Her various past retail jobs had acquainted her well with those procedures. Shannon promised her that she would be working the front end only. Not back in the bakery. Although Mari would be welcome to come and learn about the process if she felt so inclined and was careful.

Mari was looking forward to spending an entire summer at the beach. Even with the looming stress of working on a new book and her newfound temporary employment. A home near the shore was next on her wish list for her future book royalties. Something to escape to or even make a more permanent getaway one day. It would be a good experience to see if she could manage the chaos of the crowds during the summer months if she ever decided to live there full-time.

Being around people triggered her anxiety. She was able to put on a friendly face for crowds at events and book signings, but it always took a lot out of her. The idea of working in a crowded bakery on the weekends was something she was not looking forward to. The sheer fact that she was doing it in return for her free use of a beach condo was the only thing that made it tolerable. She was praying that she would not be too mentally burnt out. That the work days would leave her with nothing left to give to her writing.

She arrived early in the week. There was a need to get acclimated to the thought of not having her typical home for the summer. Staying in the condo required some mental adjustments to her comfort level. The first few nights in a new place were always restless as her mind and body became used to the noises and the space. This gentle ease into her new routine would give her anxiety a chance to ease and rest after the initial freakout.

Shannon had insisted that Mari work in the bakery on Saturday morning to get a taste of how busy it would be during the summer. It was not the usual busyness of a summer day, but it did have a steady stream of people for the Memorial Day holiday. While it was more crowded than Mari had been hoping for, it was a good way to get acclimated on what to expect.

The morning rush had finally waned, and it was dipping into the afternoon. Shannon had directed Mari to clear out the empty trays of items and stack them so her husband, Luke, could wash them. In the back, he had started the hefty task of removing the dirty mixers and bowls for the next load in the dishwasher. He did as much as he could for tomorrow's prep so they could get started on the arduous task of baking first thing.

As Mari busied herself, there was a peculiar man staring at her from behind the counter. She had not noticed him right away. She wondered how long he had been standing there with his cerulean blue eyes locked on the back of her head.

"Uh…can I help you?"

There was an uncomfortable silence as his eyes blinked back at her. Maybe he didn't speak English. Or she had caught him off guard. He looked a bit rough around the edges with an effortlessly tousled quaff of auburn hair and a beard to match. It was a stark contrast to his wrinkled dress shirt over an old college t-shirt. His tortoiseshell glasses topped off his rather professor-meets-overworked-college-senior sort of vibe. If it wasn't for the off-putting first impression, she would have considered him attractive.

The quiet was growing more uncomfortable by the second and Mari's anxiety began to bubble up in her throat. Was he there to rob the place? Stalk someone?

"Ben! You're late today." The man finally moved. His gaze shifted over to Shannon with her bright greeting. He didn't smile but gave her a modest tilt of his head in greeting. "The usual?"

"Yes, please." He spoke in such a soft tone that Mari had an entire inner dialogue on the fact if he even had said anything at all. Did she detect some sort of foreign accent? She stole a few glances here and there as she went back to busying herself with pulling the empty trays. He seemed nervous as his hand fidgeted with the watch on the wrist of his left hand.

His eyes suddenly met her curious ones through the glass display case, and it sent Mari's heart racing. For what reason, she had no idea. Perhaps it was the thought of him catching her as a nosy voyeur. Or he had pinned her as his next victim as a serial killer.

With the harsh crinkling of a paper bag, their awkward staring contest ended. Shannon had set aside his usual croissant and lemon scone from the bustle of the weekend morning rush. She waved him off with her trademark warm smile before putting his money in the cash register.

"Who the hell was that?" Mari asked with a cautious side-eye toward her friend as soon as the bell stopped jingling from his exit.

Glancing up, Shannon laughed with a dismissive wave of her hand. "Oh, that's Ben. The librarian."

"For what, the mentally deranged?"

The elaborate snort that Shannon let loose made even Mari crack up. Her friend shook her head as she laughed, wiping some powdered sugar off the counter.

"Yeah…he's a bit…odd. And that's putting it mildly." Tossing the rag into the sink, she dried her hands down the front of her apron. "He's the librarian at the island library. Down on 32nd. It's the perfect profession for him. He doesn't really need to talk. And he doesn't."

Mari narrowed her eyes in perplexed thought as she continued with her task. Even with it being the first Saturday of the unofficial start of summer, only a few treats remained. Shannon hadn't been wrong in the fact that she would need the extra help. The day had breezed by with only the three of them in the shop. Mari was ready to get off her feet and take a shower.

"Do you think I can call it a day?" Mari asked, hoping that Shannon would send her back up to the apartment.

"What? Oh my god, yes! Sorry, girl. I got all caught up in the fun." Shannon grinned and Mari shot her a look. "Come on, it's better having you here. Trust me." Her eyes were overdramatic as she tossed her gaze in the direction of the kitchen. "You're more fun than Mr. Boss Man," she said in a hushed whisper.

"I heard that," Luke said with a smirk that was quirking up into a smile. Sauntering into the room he wrapped his arm around Shannon's waist and pulled her in for a kiss. "You're lucky I love you. Well…and lucky that your parents own the place. Or else I'd have to fire you for your attitude."

"Shut it, mop boy." Shannon teased right back with a hearty pat on his butt. He slipped Mari a quick wink as he disappeared back into the kitchen. Mari snorted in amusement as Shannon laughed to herself.

The two of them acted more like best friends than traditional sort of lovers. They married eight years ago, and they still seemed like flirtatious teenagers. New love was different from older, more established love. Yet they still had that initial attraction. They made it seem like there was an effortless comfort between them.

"Same time tomorrow?" Mari piped up, distracting Shannon from her stare in her husband's direction.

"Huh? Oh yes! 7:45. It's not like you have to walk far."

Mari nodded with a laugh as she took off her apron and hung it up on the wall by the kitchen. Saying her goodbye to Luke, she slipped out of the bakery and into the warm sun. The private entrance to the bakery apartment was up an exterior wooden staircase to the rear of the building. She was making her way down to the corner to the side street when she saw him.

Ben was sitting across the street on a bench along the tree-lined street. He was eating his bakery selection with his nose in a book. His attention seemed focused on the book. Except for his eyes. His gaze was staring right at her. Mari felt a flush rise up all the way to her ears. His gaze was unrelenting as if the sheer intensity was trying to read the transcript of her soul. It made a shiver go up her spine. It wasn't a nefarious feeling, but it was a peculiar one.

Shaking her head to dispel her thoughts, she turned and hurried down the side street. As she reached the staircase, she cast one last glance back at Ben. His head had turned to follow her. Shannon had dismissed him as being harmless, albeit a bit unusual. Unusual sounded only like the tip of the iceberg.

Chapter Four

"Motherfucker!" Spat Mari in frustration at the spinning web browser. It was Tuesday and her first day off after the busy Memorial Day weekend in the bakery. With her first full week at the beach, she was going to dive head-first into her book. Or at least attempt to do so. Unfortunately, the internet was an inconsiderate foe on top of her writer's block.

The internet issue, that she had hoped was temporary, proved to be an incessant nuisance. How the hell was she supposed to get any research done? Sure, she could write, but having to keep referring to her phone to look up information was becoming annoying. She liked to completely unplug from social media and all calls and texts. Bringing her phone into the mix was screwing up her writing Feng shui. Mari needed reliable internet and a comfortable place to write.

There had to be a coffee shop or a Starbucks or something around the island. Shifting through her memory recall she couldn't think of anything off the top of her head and grumbled. The coffee shops on the island were restaurants. Despite the good food and coffee, they didn't exactly have the best environment to write in. She needed to go drive around the island and look. At the very least she would end up with a decent cup of coffee for her efforts.

Mari grabbed her keys and purse and shuffled down the back steps to her parked car. Her azure eyes surfed up and down the street for the perplexing human that was Ben the librarian. He unnerved her, like a complex brain teaser she needed to crack. He had shown up on Sunday as well, all around the same time. It was always after the buzz of the morning crowds had dissipated. Each time Mari felt those intense blue eyes staring her down with nary a word in her direction.

The more she thought about him the more she was becoming intrigued by him. He would make an excellent villain or even a haggard wizard character in one of her fantasy novels. It wouldn't be so awful if she could run into him again. Ben was beginning to captivate her. It would be worth the discomfort to conduct more of an in-depth character study.

In her mission to find suitable Wi-Fi, all Mari ended up with was a delicious caramel latte from a shop in Stone Harbor, the next town over. It was already mid-morning, and she hadn't written for longer than an hour. The mission was still at hand. She needed to find a suitable and quiet place to write for a prolonged period of time.

As she was driving back towards Avalon, it hit her.
Duh, the library.

Mari groaned as her forehead hit the steering wheel at the red light. Well of course that made sense. A library would have everything that she needed. But it would have Ben. Despite her desperate desire to stay on schedule and write, she was not exactly looking forward to running into him on purpose. Especially after the weekend of awkward stares and silence with their fleeting interactions. He might even think that she's stalking or obsessed with him. He could be one of those odd lives-in-his-mother's-basement types. Although the island didn't have any basements. At least he had that going for him.

Pulling into the lot, Mari parked and turned off her car before grabbing her laptop bag, purse, and coffee. The sandy-colored brick building was bright and welcoming. Its façade made way for large windows to offer plenty of light. Even the metal lettering and logo lining the entrance were beachy and fun to fit with the vibe of the island.

She was hoping that she could avoid Ben at all costs. Perhaps he had an office that he liked to hide in. Or maybe he was off today. The worst-case scenario would be him sitting at the front desk and spotting her as she walked in. No matter what, this was her last resort to get any writing done while spending the summer at the beach. It was this or go home. Or well…pay an astronomical cell phone bill and abuse her phone's hot spot. The library seemed like the most painless, albeit awkward option.

Mari pulled the door open, sure to keep her head down and avoid any eye contact with the odd librarian. Casting her eyes about, the coast was clear. She made a beeline for the opposite end of the library in the furthest corner that happened to have a table.

Mari dropped her bags with relief down onto the table as she let out the breath she had been holding. Casting a wary look around to see that the coast was clear, she began to unload her laptop and plopped onto the seat. It wasn't the most comfortable chair she had ever sat in. At least it would keep her upright and more focused on work instead of zoning out. Mari opened her laptop and booted it up, anxious to see what her connectivity would be like in here. She breathed a sigh of relief as her laptop connected to the free Wi-Fi.

Popping in her earbuds, Mari set to work. That morning she had at least managed to add a bit to the rough summary she had written in the weeks before. That was until the internet started being a jerk. The library's internet wasn't as fast as her one at home, but it was lightyears better than what the apartment had.

Her abrupt change in venue took her some time to find her groove. She picked the most upbeat playlist on her phone. Anything so she could remain alert and focused to at least get more work done before the library closed. Her typing turned more furious as the day continued. Things were coming together. Slowly, but surely.

She reached out for her coffee cup as she read over the summary that she had written for chapter twelve. Despite it being the remnants of her now cold coffee, she was desperate for the caffeine and brought it to her lips.

"No food or drink," Ben said in crisp warning. His voice *did* have an accent. It sounded like he was from some region of the UK. England maybe? Scotland? It was loud enough that she had heard it, despite her earbuds. The abrupt words startled Mari, causing her to lose her grip on her coffee cup, sending her fumbling for it.

There wasn't much more than a sip left although the rest of the contents ended up on her lap.

"S-sorry…" Mari muttered. Her heart was high up in her throat, choking her with her sudden burst of fright and anxiety. Her eyes darted over to him as he wandered away from her. It felt like a teacher had scolded her for breaking a school rule.

Today he looked more put together. He must have run a comb through his hair at least. The collared dress shirt was crisp from an iron along with his khakis. He had rolled up the sleeves of his shirt to his elbows. To her surprise, his forearms showed off subtle definition.

What the actual fuck am I doing.
I should not be checking out the town weirdo.

But there she was, in a public library, leaning back in her chair to watch his rather nice ass walk around the corner. Turning away, Mari pressed her forehead into her hand and propped her elbow up on the table. It had to have been that extra shot of espresso in her latte that afternoon that was making her a little loopy. Or it was eye fatigue from staring at the computer screen too long that day. A slow drive back to the apartment and some fresh air would do her lapse of judgment some good.

She made a desperate attempt to collect her thoughts before she shut down her computer. There was no way that she was so lonely that she would find the off-putting librarian attractive. Mari didn't want to answer that stream of internal questioning as she shoved her computer into her bag. There was still a grouping of drying coffee blotches along her thigh and the bottom of her shirt. There wasn't much she could do about it now as she made her way out of the library.

Mari kept her eyes on the floor as she briskly made her way to the front entrance. With any luck, she could avoid Ben once again. The glass double doors were in sight, and she reached out to put her hand on the handle. Only one more move to push her way out into the warm breeze of freedom.

"You're Mari Quay." The statement was simple but confident. It was in that same crooning accent that she had tried so hard to avoid on her way out. She should have ignored him. Although the way she paused in her cringe at the door made him assume that he was correct. Ben glued his intense stare on her from his position behind the counter.

Instead of trying to remain anonymous, Ben had singled her out. That could have been why he kept staring at her in the bakery every day. Maybe it was because he recognized her but couldn't figure out from where. Of course he would know who she is. Almost every library in the country had a display of her small collection of books in some form or fashion. National bestselling books were always in demand.

"Ya got me." Mari conceded in her best playful tone. She shrugged her shoulders and slowly turned to him. His gaze never changed as their eyes met. Those blue eyes were still intense and rabid in their study of her. He had a weird habit of making her skin crawl and yet her body felt warm all over. It was a perplexing feeling.

"I thought so." There was that awkward silence again.

"So…is that all? Or are you going to give me a lecture on bringing in coffee?" Mari had meant it as a joke to ease the uncomfortable tension, but Ben didn't even flinch.

"The library does not allow food and drink inside."

What was with this dude?

"Yeah…I got that. It won't happen again."

"I'm Ben McGregor." His informal introduction came out of nowhere and Mari blinked. He had blurted it out for no particular reason. Where did this man learn how to talk to people? Especially as a librarian? His customer service skills with the people who used the library had to be better than this.

"Um…hi?" She was doing her best to remain polite. He could be a rabid fan who was starstruck in her presence. Considering how he had let his name tumble forth out of the blue. He hadn't managed to scare her off quite yet. "Do you…like my books? Or…something?"

The sheepish nod and wide eyes only confirmed Mari's suspicion. She couldn't help but laugh. She enjoyed having fans but meeting them in person was completely different. Something that she didn't exactly care for in unexpected encounters.

"Ah well…nice to meet you, Ben. I hope you don't mind me using the library this summer to write. But I really need to head out." She didn't bother to wait to see or hear his response. Mari pushed open the door with the side of her body, slipping out into the vestibule, and then into the late-day sun.

Ben's eyes widened with excitement at her admission. His mouth dropped open in hopes of saying something else, but she had left. Admitting he was a fan may have tinged a far too awkward. Even a bit into stalker-ish territory and he kicked himself for doing so. At least Mari Quay would be back.

Chapter Five

Mari found herself sitting in her car in front of the library the next morning. If the weather hadn't gotten so hot, she would have considered sitting in her car to write. She would have pirated off the library's Wi-Fi that happened to seep into the parking area along the building. The other option was to leave her car idle but that was unnecessary stress on her car. Not when there was a suitable building to use right in front of her. She would have to swallow her pride, along with the rest of her coffee, and enter the library.

Chugging her latte, she dropped the empty cup back into her car's cup holder with a sigh. There was no use prolonging the inevitable. Not if she needed to stick to some kind of schedule. She had already received an email from Faith asking when she could get an ETA on the first draft. Mari was not even close to offering up such a timeline yet.

With her bag gathered from her car, she adjusted the strap on her arm with a hefty sigh. Why she was being so apprehensive over something as silly as a human interaction was beyond her. She had met tons of fans in the past that were almost as awkward as Ben McGregor. But never had she submitted herself to being in the same building with them for days on end either.

Slipping through the vestibule's doors, she hesitantly opened the interior one. A statuesque Ben greeted her in an almost monotone from behind the front desk. Even though she was half-expecting him, his stoic stillness still startled her. It was as if he had been waiting for her to arrive. There was a subtle flex of his brows that could have almost been misconstrued for delight.

"Mari. Good morning." At least he was courteous.

"Hi, Ben." She offered a small bob of her head in greeting before turning to make a beeline for her table in the back corner. He would have to go out of his way to bother her there. But Mari had a feeling that he was going to do just that. Tomorrow she would have to bring her more obvious headphones if he chanced to disturb her.

Mari set to work setting up her writing home base for the day. Booting up her laptop, she laid out a small tablet of paper and a pencil to jot down any notes. The sun shone through the window. It promised to be a welcome accompaniment to her, hopefully, productive day.

Glancing around, she jammed her earbuds into her ears. She plopped down in the wooden chair as she scrolled through her playlists. Something upbeat, a mix of pop-hit love songs to get the right vibe going. Any sort of inspiration would be welcome at this point, no matter how shallow and reaching it might be.

As for right now, the coast was clear. Mari leaned in over her computer and began reviewing where she had left off. The abrupt interruption of Ben yesterday had thrown her out of her grove. She couldn't concentrate on continuing to work after the fact. Now she needed to spend time falling back into the mindset that she had been in before Ben interrupted her.

Ben kept his distance. He didn't dare chance to come within her line of sight. He always lingered behind and watched her work without a sound. She was rather expressive as she sat there, even when he could only see the back of her. It was obvious when a good song came on. Her head would bob to the beat, or her hands would go up into the air with a little dance move from the comfort of her seat. She seemed a little peculiar.

Mari sat with a hunch over her laptop. Her brow furrowed as her fingers tangled in the hair around the crown of her head. It was as if she managed to stare long enough, it would bring words to her brain. But nothing was coming to her. No matter how hard she tried to bring something, anything to fruition.

"What are you listening to?"

Dammit, all to hell.

Glancing up from the corner of her perturbed gaze, Mari spotted Ben standing too close to her. His curiosity had sounded more like a statement than a question. It sent her mind reeling with perplexity. She scrambled to sit up into a more ladylike position and thumbed the volume down on her phone.

"2000s Pop."

"Oh."

If all their exchanges were going to be this awkward, she would need to reevaluate her situation. There had to be a more beneficial location for Mari to find more favorable free Wi-Fi. Even if it meant going far inland. The quiet had settled in and yet he still stood there, looking at her. She didn't want to be rude, but she didn't exactly want him to be hovering over her either. Her brain was in overload with endless choices on how she could best get out of the situation.

"Do you...like music?"

"I do."

Where the hell did this man learn how to converse? He couldn't even carry on a half-decent conversation. His answers were short and unreciprocated. He made no effort to further the conversation. She opened her mouth to at least attempt to continue their chat, but he was already headed back in the direction of the front desk.

Mari turned in her seat to follow him, her jaw slack and her mouth hanging open. Ben the librarian was an unyielding paradox. If he ever managed to smile, he would at least be approachable, handsome even. But the well-trimmed bearded face remained in an endless and stoic impasse.

If he would leave her alone all day, Mari could at least get deep enough into her groove to finish a chapter or two. But no, he had to bug her. Over such trivial things with such random and shallow questions. Nothing of which was important enough to interrupt her over.

Yet they continued. One or two, daily at first, then it increased to more and more interactions. They were still sufficiently awkward but less so as time went on. By the end of the second week, he had managed to get out four somewhat lengthy sentences in one day. It was hardly a conversation, but he was getting there.

Even with the daily distractions, Mari had written a few chapters. It was nowhere near where she needed to be, but it was at least some semblance of a decent start to her new project. The word count might even get Faith off her back for the time being. She had even begun to mentally prepare herself for Ben's daily interruptions. Anything to make them feel less jarring and unexpected.

One day she was certain that Ben had started to wear a new cologne. Or he started to wear cologne. Mari had taken special note because he smelled divine. The enchanting scent was something reminiscent of a mountainside at dusk. There was no other way to describe it. She had actually wanted him to come and bother her so she could get another enticing whiff of it. He had also begun to wear a tie here and there and even pulled off a tailored sport coat one day. If she had been a ballsy woman, she would have teased him about dressing up for her.

Mari was a difficult woman to read, and Ben was unsure if anything he had done had any effect on her. Still, she continued to return to the library at least. Even though she visibly bristled whenever he interrupted her typing mid-sentence. He just wanted to talk to her, but the words tumbled forth with his terrible timing and from the anxiety he felt around her. But maybe, in due time, he would be comfortable enough around her to ask her out.

Chapter Six

By the third week, Mari had descended into the vicious dark hallows of writer's block. It left her in a foul mood. No matter what she tried, the words were not flowing. When she did manage to write something, it ended up being terrible. She deleted words almost as quickly as she typed them. She had contemplated not going to the library just so she didn't have to deal with Ben's pointless questions. But there was a tiny part of her that actually sort of looked forward to the attention now.

It sounded so awful and desperate. Mari was apparently so deprived of attention that she began to crave the uncomfortableness that was Ben McGregor. She had to be going insane. This book was making her insane. That was the only explanation.

She was locked in a debate of deciding to go to the library and attempt to write or admit defeat for the day. It was her first day off for the week. Tuesday and Wednesday were the days that the bakery closed, and she was free to write all day and night if she wished. She despised letting all this limited time to go waste.

It was already well into the afternoon when Mari managed to venture out in an attempt to write something. She had coaxed herself from the apartment with the promise of a fountain soda, a much-needed caffeine boost. Driving with the windows down and the sweet sea air managed to rouse her a bit more. She apparently needed to get outside for some fresh air and a change of scenery more often.

Mari set up shop at her usual table in the back. She had slipped into the library unnoticed as Ben was not at the front counter. Slumping down in her seat, she opened up her laptop and frowned at the same screen that had been mocking her all day. Leaning back in her chair, she prayed to the writing gods for any kind of inspiration. From there she settled in to try writing at least something, no matter how bad it was.

"Mari?" She stirred and made some sort of off-putting grumble of a noise. Ben had been attempting to rouse the sleeping woman from her slump over her laptop. It was already ten minutes past closing and he was eager to get home. He luckily happened to look up from gathering his things when he saw her spread out, and unconscious, at her usual table.

"Mari?" His hand trembled something terrible as he timidly reached out. It took all the strength he could muster to lay his hand on her shoulder. The shaking of his hand was enough to rouse her. "A-are you all right...?"

Blinking, Mari eased herself to sit up. Her vision was blurry from sleep as she attempted to take in her surroundings and figure out what year it was. There was no way that she had been that tired. Certainly not tired enough to fall asleep in the middle of the public library.

She startled viciously as her gaze shifted to the sight of Ben standing next to her. The adrenaline from her surprise brought her to full consciousness.

"Holy shit! Ben! Fuck, dammit." Mari spat as she rubbed her eyes under her smudged glasses, trying to hide from her embarrassment. "I wasn't snoring or anything was I?"

Ben couldn't help the chuckle at her flustered outburst and question. He shook his head with the negative. But that was not what Mari cared about at that exact moment. Did he just...*laugh*? And it wasn't just any laugh, it was a smooth and crooning amused chuckle that simmered with his accent. In her flustered state that was the last thing she needed.

"No. It's…past closing. I almost locked you in for the night." Ben realized that his hand was still on her shoulder and quickly removed it, hiding it behind his back.

"Are you fucking kidding me?" Mari ran an exasperated hand through her mussed hair as she began the scramble to collect her things. Ben's blue gaze stuck on her tousled locks.

Clearing his throat to avoid the already blooming blush, he took a step back in a vain effort to clear his thoughts. "Are you okay?"

The dry crisp break of a laugh that tumbled from her mouth conveyed how close to hysteria she felt.

"No…" Mari whimpered in defeat with a sigh and dropped her head into her hand, propping her elbow on the edge of the table. "This fucking project… It's going to be the end of me." Throwing her head back, she tried to mentally put on her big girl panties. Blinking away tears, she shot Ben a fake smile. "It's not been a productive writing day. Days." She corrected herself with a huff. "But the show must go on, right? No rest for the weary writer."

"Let's go for drinks." He blurted without thinking. Clamping his eyes shut he groaned internally at his sudden word vomit. Sure, now he had the balls to ask her out. In the midst of her being emotional and stressed out. Oh well, at least it was out in the open now. "My treat." There was a poor attempt at a crooked yet reassuring smile.

His words had caught her off-guard. Did he ask her out? No, that was silly. He was just trying to be a supportive random semi-stranger. Fuck it. A night out with alcohol sounded good. Even if she wasn't much of a drinker.

"Really?" Mari perked up a bit as she wiped her eye free of stray tears with the heel of her hand. "That-that would be…nice actually."

"Oh, I unders-… Wait, what?" Ben almost had to do a double take. He expected a firm rebuttal. "Y-you actually want to?"

"Yeah, fuck it," Mari stated firmly as she stood. She shoved her laptop, paper tablet, and pencils into her bag haphazardly. "Let's go before I change my mind."

Ben nodded as he stepped back for Mari to follow him out. Glancing over his shoulder, he nervously made his way to the front door. This wasn't a date. This was just two people going out for drinks. That's it. That's all it was. Drinks out to de-stress. Nothing more.

Locking up, Ben cleared his throat as he had to figure out the next part of the spontaneous plans.

"Do you want me to drive or…?"

"Uh…no I can meet you there. Where are we going?"

Ben's eyes shifted as he tried to think on his feet. He wasn't much of a drinker, so the bar scene wasn't well-known to him. The only bars he knew of were in Sea Isle. They were a bit wilder and earmarked more for the heavier serial drinkers. The two of them needed something with more of a calming, restaurant vibe.

"Uh…the Wind Drift?"

Mari had to hand it to Ben. The Wind Drift was one of the premier venues on the island. Good vibe, good food, and it was even on the beach. The idea of a night out was sounding better by the minute.

"Good choice." Shooting him a grin, Mari slipped into her car and closed the door. Ben watched her from the driver's side of his car, lost in some sort of hysteria and dream-like state. He needed to keep his cool if this whole endeavor was going to turn out half-decent.

Mari was the first to arrive. The parking lot wasn't too packed as it was still early in the season for most of the vacationers. Peak season started the following week and Mari had been dreading the chaos that was about to unfold. This night of drinking was coming at the perfect time.

They walked up the steps to the front entrance of the restaurant. It was on the second floor so patrons would have a clearer view of the ocean above the sand dunes. The place was about half full and had plenty of room at the bar. There was more than enough room for the two of them, so they didn't have to feel overwhelmed by the crowd alone. The only thing they had to worry about was the other person in their presence.

"Forgive me for any stupid shit that may come out of my mouth tonight," Mari warned Ben as the bartender sauntered off to get their drinks. He glanced at her with a quiet nervous bit of laughter. Determined now, she wanted to get a full-fledged laugh out of him before the end of the night. Even if she wasn't sober enough to remember it. "I'm serious. Alcohol and I don't get along. I get loud and talkative. The complete opposite of me." Ben snorted as he leaned forward onto the bar with his elbows.

"Duly noted. I'm sure you'll be fine." He reassured her as the bartender handed them their bottles. Reaching out, he fingered the slick glass of the neck of the Corona in thought. Leaning back, he grasped the slender neck in his hand. Turning to Mari, he offered up his beer. "Here's to words that flow as freely as the alcohol on my tab tonight."

A brow cocked high on Mari's forehead as she turned to Ben in muted surprise. His words were eloquent and rather humorous. There was no way she was turning down a unique cheer like that. Grabbing her hard cider bottle, she lifted it up. Tipping it forward, she clinked it against his before bringing it to her lips and taking a long swig. His eyes watched her, transfixed, as she swallowed down the alcohol. Clenching his eyes shut, he reminded himself to not stare and be awkward. He lifted his bottle and took a quick swig of the golden nectar. It swirled around the lime stuck in the neck of the bottle as it descended into his mouth.

It took Mari two full bottles of the hard cider on an empty stomach for the words to flow as loosely as she had warned. She was so carefree and tipsy now and about to start her third bottle. Ben watched her with intrigued interest. He had taken the fortitude to order them a cheese board to share. At least she could eat some food to absorb all that alcohol. He was sure to take his time with his beer. Even though his nerves were shot, he wanted to have a clear head and his wits about him.

Ben had finally relaxed as it seemed that Mari wasn't going anywhere soon. She had been regaling him of the woes of being a popular published author. He had no idea how jaded the industry could be behind the curtain. She provided such a candid hashing out of the darker details behind the scenes. Of what exactly it took to get all the books in his library that he surrounded himself with every day.

"Do you have any idea how hard it is to write a book with thousands of people breathing down your neck? It's impossible!" Mari hadn't been wrong about getting loud with her increased alcohol consumption. Ben had to continue to hush her. It came with a chuckle whenever she got passionate about something. "Some days I hate my life. I really do."

"D-don't say that. You're...very gifted." Ben offered timidly with a blush to the apples of his cheeks. Mari reached out and clasped his shoulder in thanks. Her face was trembling, on the borderline of tears.

"You're so fucking nice. Has anyone told you that?" The redness in his cheeks increased and he looked away for a moment as her touch lingered. "But I can't fucking do this. I can't write this book."

"O-of course you can. Y-you're a best-selling author. Anything should be a piece of cake for you."

"But not this one!" Mari whined with an overdose of drama as she dragged her hand down his arm to slap it back onto the bar.

"Why not?"

"Because!"

"Because why?"

"Because! I've never been in a real relationship!" The words tumbled out in a hushed jumble as tears pooled in the corners of her eyes. "How can you fucking write something when you've never actually done it? How do you convey that sort of...emotion? You can research it all you want. But unless it's something you've actually experienced...it doesn't come off...authentic."

Ben sat back, startled. He hadn't expected anything like this soul-baring sort of conversation that she had dropped on him all at once. The confession had left a shocked expression on his face.

"W-well…um…why don't you uh…date someone?" He offered, even though he knew that it was rather unhelpful advice.

"Don't you think I've fucking already tried that? I mean…I've dated guys. But…not like *dated*, dated. You know?"

Ben could only blink with surprise. He had to lean back away from her as she leaned forward to emphasize her point. He did sort of understand what she was getting at. The dating game had not been easy. In school, he was lanky and awkward. It wasn't until he came to the States that he managed to get some interest from the opposite sex on account of his accent. But even that wasn't enough for most women to get past his off-putting awkwardness and quiet.

"Yeah…I mean no! Er well, yes but with women."

Mari let loose this raucous snort of a laugh. It made him take pause before he burst out laughing in reply. It was so unladylike, but it was such a hilarious outburst of a reaction that he couldn't help himself. Watching her make an ass of herself made him feel more and more comfortable around her. At least she wasn't getting up to leave due to sheer boredom, as most of his past dates had done.

"Wait. You? You have trouble getting the ladies? Nooooo…" Her reply came out oozing with sarcasm and he couldn't help but shrug his shoulders. "Come on, the whole distinguished professor look? It's such a kink for some women." Ben outright flushed.

"A-ah well…maybe…" He stuttered out, avoiding her gaze.

"Show a little more confidence and you could be a panty-dropper."

The fluster of her words went down his spine as he flushed a vibrant pink straight up to his ears. The hue of his skin almost matched the red in his hair.

"Ah…no. I-I've never really had a chance to…pursue any sort of meaningful relationship." They were two peas in an awkward pod. Two helpless individuals who have not had the best luck in the dating game.

"Fuck." Mari groaned. "Why do we have to fucking suck so bad? What's wrong with us?"

Ben couldn't help but laugh with a shake of his head. How was it that they were so awful at dating and keeping the interest of a partner? They were both grown-ass adults and had never learned how to have a normal relationship.

It was then that a completely absurd thought crossed his mind.

"Maybe we could…practice with each other? You know…like a learning exercise. Figure out what we are doing wrong. Then report back with an impartial response from the opposite sex."

There was a prolonged silence as Mari tried to comprehend his idea in her alcohol-addled state.

"Holy shit." Mari slowly turned to him. Her eyes were wild with excitement. "That's…a great idea!"

Ben's eyes went wide in horror.

"Wait…what? No, I didn't mean-"

"We can go on practice dates and then give each other notes!" Mari outright squealed and waved her hands with excitement. "Oh my god, Ben. You are a genius!" Her eyes started to dart around as she mentally tried to concoct some sort of plan. "This might actually save my ass with my book!"

He had boxed himself into quite a corner now. Why did he have to blurt out that insane idea? Of all the times he actually had the courage to carry on a decent conversation with a woman, he had to go and say something completely stupid.

Mari downed the last bit of her third hard cider before slamming it back down onto the bar. His eyes gave her a cautious once-over as she attempted to steady herself on her barstool. Perhaps this wasn't so terrible after all. Maybe Mari will be too drunk to remember this conversation tomorrow.

"Bartender, another round!" There was a crack in his voice as he called out. Another drink for the both of them might make them forget this entire conversation had happened. One more drink could wipe this night from existence. Then tomorrow they could go back to the same gifted woman writer, perturbed by the same nosy awkward librarian.

Chapter Seven

Mari was thankful that it was Wednesday. It was Wednesday, wasn't it? Trying to figure out the day of the week, so early in the morning, with a splitting headache was no easy task. What the hell had she done the night before?

Squinting, she rolled over onto her side and grabbed her phone.

11 am?!?

What in the actual fuck did she do last night?

There were no calls or texts from Shannon, so she deducted that it was at least Thursday. Thank goodness for that because she was not going anywhere fast. Writing anything today was going to be a difficult task altogether.

Did she go out drinking? Wait…she did…but who with?

Oh fuck.

Ben McGregor had asked her out for drinks.

And she had said *yes*.

And she had drank so fucking much.

Shit.

This was bad. So bad. What nonsense did she word vomit in her inebriated state? Better yet, had Ben even managed to utter more than a few sentences to her? Offering to take her out to drinks was one of the last things she had ever expected from him. He didn't seem like the type that would have the guts to do so. Let alone actually stay to sit and drink with her over the course of the evening.

Easing herself up out of bed, she stumbled into the bathroom for antacids and painkillers. She hastily chewed down the chalky tablets with a dry heave. An entire glass of questionable tap water washed down the painkillers. Sticking her tongue out in a dramatic gag, she wandered into the kitchen. Mari needed food and more hydration if she was going to attempt to accomplish any writing that day.

Leaning against the counter, she started to chug the sports drink that she had pulled from the fridge. Having them handy was perfect for the days she would get too engrossed in work. She would get so involved in writing and forget to hydrate. In the end, she would wind up with an excruciating headache. Or they were useful for when she managed to drink herself into a stupor. The latter was rare. But she was thankful to her not-hungover self for having the bottles for the days of her poor life choices.

Her brain was still a groggy mess. She rubbed her eyes in a vain effort to dispel it. What the hell drove her to drink last night? She was usually a light drinker. She always called it a night after two hard ciders, tops. Although she was certain she had lost count after the fourth one. The bill that Ben had at the end of the end had more than likely not been a pretty one. Didn't he also order them food? She must have looked like a complete raving mess to bribe her silence with food.

Wait, how the hell did she even get home last night? There was no way she would have been stupid enough to drive home. Plus, Ben didn't seem like the kind of person to let her make an idiotic choice like that. At least Mari was certain he wouldn't do such a thing.

As her eyes moved about the apartment, she saw that her shoes were on the tray by the door. Her purse hung on a hook. All the things that she was sure she couldn't have managed to pull off if she had been as drunk as she thought she had been.

Her phone buzzed from the depths of her purse hanging on the hooks by the front door. She jumped and slapped a hand to her sternum, trying to calm her already-addled heart. Shuffling over, she managed to inelegantly fish it out and unlock it.

It was a text from Ben McGregor.

How did she get his number?

Wait, how did he get *her* number?

How are you feeling this morning?

Mari stared at her phone in disbelief. To her relief, it was the only message in the text conversation. At least she had no embarrassing drunk texts that she had to worry about. Should she even bother responding to him? The text seemed harmless enough.

> I've been better
> How the hell did I get home last night?

I drove you
I hope you don't mind that I let myself in with your key
You weren't exactly steady on your feet
I worried that you might fall going up the stairs

Ben's texts came in fast and furious. They were the complete opposite of his usual conversation style. Text messages might be the secret to getting inside his head. Because normal methods of conversation were not getting her anywhere. Had he managed to talk more while at the bar?

Rereading his texts again, her heart leaped into her throat. He helped her get inside her apartment. Did that mean he helped her to bed too? She was still wearing her clothes from yesterday. But he had taken the time to put her shoes and her purse back in their place.

The small acts of kindness gave her pause. Sure, Ben was weird, but he seemed to have a heart of gold hidden under all his unsettling awkwardness. The entire exchange was sobering her up as her mind tumbled with the implications. Why did he have to cause her so much mental confusion?

The painkillers finally started to ease their way through her body. She could feel her mental fog struggling to clear. Mari tried to retrace her steps and recall the conversation that they had last night. She hoped that she didn't say anything too off-putting or stupid. Although, since he texted her, she assumed that she hadn't.

Finally able to walk without the room spinning, Mari made her way into her bathroom, stripping her clothes along the way. Every part of her still reeked of alcohol and it aggravated her already woozy stomach. As she stepped into the shower, the warm water felt soothing over her tired muscles. She had been carrying so much stress on her shoulders with the book.

The book.

Her book.

The current bane of her existence.

What the hell was she going to do about her book? How was she ever going to be able to write about love, romance, and relationships when she never had anything resembling any of that? She did want it, or at least some semblance of it. As much as she liked her space and quiet, there were times when she wanted to share a holiday or a special event with someone other than herself. Not to mention that she had to replace her little battery-operated friends every few months or so due to…*overuse*.

Some attention from the opposite sex would be welcomed. Well, the good kind of attention. Knowing her luck, she'd wish for attention and only receive unwanted advances from creepy basement dwellers.

Something began to resonate, deep within the recesses of her memory. Why did it ring a bell? This train of thought…hadn't she talked about it recently? The person she usually chatted with about guy issues was Shannon. But they had barely said much outside of the shop lately. Mari would die before she brought it up to Faith. So…who did she talk about relationship woes with? The only person she had a conversation with of late was Ben.

Fuck.

It was Ben.

In her drunken stupor and with loose lips she had admitted to him that she sucked at relationships. Why did she have to go out drinking with him? Then go and admit such a dirty secret to a man that, with tweaking, could make her panties hit the floor.

But what had Ben said in response to her embarrassing past? He didn't laugh, not that she could remember. There was something…something on the tip of her tongue. It resonated with her drunk self. Was it an idea? An idea for her book?

Mari's fingers tangled in her hair, a futile attempt to file through the events of last night. To get to the one nugget that actually could be useful. The thing must have been something completely absurd that only her drunk self could have appreciated.

The water had gone cold, and Mari grew frustrated. Why couldn't she remember? If she was on better terms with Ben, she would have texted him to ask. Although maybe he wouldn't remember either? She wasn't exactly sure how much he drank and when he sobered up. This sort of thing wouldn't bother her so much if it wasn't something maybe vital to her project.

Stepping out of the shower, she threw the towel over her head and dried her hair. The sudden jostling of her brain finally did it.

She remembered.

Followed by a sudden rush of choking anxiety.

Date each other?

For the sake of her book?

What kind of idea is that?

Absurd, but brilliant.

Mari was all about doing research for her books. Research for information and experiences helped her convey emotion to her readers. This seemed…complicated, but interesting. It was far better than reading other writers' works to get an idea of love and romance. It was even better than redownloading the dating apps and giving in to that Russian Roulette nonsense again.

What harm would it do? She could very well end up with some helpful pointers. Or her awkwardness would scare Ben off. Either way, it sounded like a win to her. She could end up with some helpful tips in the dating/relationship world. Or scar Ben so much that he would leave her alone for the rest of the summer. So, all in all, not a bad idea.

Chapter Eight

Ben awoke that morning with the faintest tinge of a headache. Unlike Mari, he could recall every moment of their time together from the night before. He had wanted to get completely plastered. Especially after he opened his big mouth. But after watching Mari go through her hard ciders, he held off. The off-the-wall suggestion of dating each other, to help Mari get past the creative block in her book, was such a stupid idea. Why did he have to go and blurt it out? Although to be honest, he was eager for his side of the bargain. To learn the secrets of women so that he could stop being so obscenely awkward.

He couldn't bring himself to drink any further than keeping up with his light buzz. Mari had to get back home safely and he took it upon himself to make sure of it. She had gotten more drunk than she had wanted to be. Drowning her woes in bottle after bottle of hard cider and being a complete lightweight. She had eased her usual bristle and had assumed a sort of comfortability with him.

Mari had opened up, sip by sip. He had learned so much about the world of writing and publishing. She had unloaded her stressors and woes on him. It sounded like she had been keeping all this animosity bottled up for months. All she needed was a bit of liquid courage to let it all out.

Despite the less-than-ideal night out, Ben couldn't stop thinking about it. About her. As much as he wanted to suppress the swirling emotions rising up in his stomach, he couldn't. Ben was finding himself more and more enamored with Mari. Typically when his infatuations would get to this stage, he would inadvertently do something to mess it all up.

She had looked worse for wear when he helped her get home the night before. The task of walking up the stairs after their night of drinking had worn her out. She almost fell over attempting to take her flip-flops off. Fading fast, Ben had done the only logical thing. He scooped her up in his arms and carried her to bed.

In an actual dating situation, perhaps she would have kissed him, maybe even giggled with the surprise. There would have been unspoken promises as he took her to bed. Ones that led to a night of pleasures and not letting her rouse from bed until the next morning. He felt himself grow flushed from his sudden sultry thoughts. No, he couldn't think that way about her. Not even in the least bit. As tantalizing as those thoughts were, they were hardly appropriate.

He had left her curled up and asleep alone in her own bed. On his way out, he put her shoes away on the boot tray and hung her purse up. With his final act of care, he placed her keys on the small entrance table and locked the door before shutting himself out.

For a long moment, he had stood on her front stoop and stared at the front door. It had been quite some time since he held a woman so intimately. Even though it was something completely innocent. Ben was doing his best to suppress the ache and longing he felt inside. With a sigh, he turned and headed back to his parked car. Alone. As much as he tried to dispel the thoughts, they lingered the entire way home and even as he lay in bed. Though tired as he was, his body continued to crave more contact after having the tiniest shred until he had finally managed to fall asleep, still wanting.

Arriving at work that morning, he did not expect to see Mari make her daily visit to work on her book. She had to have been nursing a killer hangover. Movement at the library's front entrance pulled him from his thoughts. He scrambled to pull together some semblance of composure. Some of the older patrons usually said hello but most ignored him. Which is how he liked it. Yet, this guest was marching right up to the front desk, with determination.

Looking up, Ben felt a jolt go up his spine. It was Mari. She looked rough with her hair in a messy bun and a dark shadow under her eyes. There was a burning question in her haggard gaze. The intensity made him take pause as he wandered out of his windowed office. The complex look on her face made him wonder if something had pissed her off.

Swallowing dryly, he stepped up to the front desk with a tremble in his voice.

"G-good morning, Mari."

"Were you serious?" There were no return pleasantries. Her question was crisp as she was on a quest to know if he was being earnest with his absurd idea or not. She needed to know the answer. The offer he had extended to her the night before had been eating her alive all morning. What he had suggested was her last resort to accomplishing something in her book. She needed any help she could get at this point.

Ben blinked blankly at her. Even after all that alcohol, there was no way that she could have remembered what he said. The one time he actually had the balls to talk to a woman and look where he ended up. Stuck in a proposed awkward dating scenario.

"Were. You. Serious?"

She had him cornered now, punctuating her words with extra emphasis in case he had not heard her the first time. He moved his shy gaze away from her intense stare and instead studied the wood grain top of the front desk. What could he say to her? That no, he wasn't serious about the "dating for science" arrangement? Or the fact that every fiber of his being was screaming for him to do it.

"Yes." Ben managed to squeak out, still refusing to meet her gaze. Her hand slapped down on the desk and startled him from his stupor. As he cautiously looked up at her, there was some kind of frenzied elation spreading across her face. Despite her drunkenness last night, Mari seemed excited about the prompt.

"Excellent. How about tonight?"

"T-t-tonight…?" Ben stuttered. Despite the enthusiasm of a woman asking him out on a date, he was not ready to follow through with it. "I-I don't know… Isn't it…soon?"

"Not when you have an agent and an editor breathing down your neck." Determined now, Mari did not back down. Gluing her feet to the carpet-tiled floor, she refused to move until he gave her confirmation. Confirmation to an agreement that they could go out on a date in their little social experiment. Her blue eyes softened a bit as her tone turned into a plea. "Come on, Ben. Please?"

The borderline begging did him in. Did him in, in more ways than one.

"O-okay. S-s-sure…we can."

A smile of relief flooded her features with delight as the stress relaxed from her shoulders. Mari looked almost like a different person without the weight that had been on her back for as long as he had known her. His hand twitched and for a moment he wanted nothing more than to pull her in for a celebratory kiss.

"You are going to save my ass if this works. I'm going to go write now!" Mari scampered off with a newfound spring in her step. Ben watched her walk off in disbelief. Did he actually have a date? A real date, with a lovely woman no less? For the second night in a row?

Yes. Yes, he did.

Chapter Nine

Dinner was already strained and awkward enough with the notion of practicing dating. Now there was the additional task of giving and receiving productive feedback on what they were doing wrong. Yet neither of them had even attempted to engage the other in an active conversation. The waiter pulled away with their drink orders and they continued to sit in utter silence.

"Should we just talk via text or what…?" Mari offered. She was getting a bit testy as Ben continued to avoid her gaze. Forgetting herself, she sighed and looked at her hands folded in her lap. "If this is going to work, we have to both at least try. And offer helpful advice to each other."

Ben finally looked up at her. His outfit was like something a man in his 50s would wear for going out to eat with his family. There was no reason to date himself so far beyond his 30s. Despite how buttoned up he was with a sweater vest and dress shirt, he still looked handsome. Even with the uneasy look in his eyes. If he could wear something a bit more appropriate for his age, Mari would have found herself much more distracted.

"Right. Talk." Ben tried to be sound and sure as he cast a quick glance back at Mari. His fingers were wrestling each other in his lap as he fretted about what to even talk about. "So…um, uh…did you…uh…write? Today?"

"A bit. Not as much as I wanted to." Casting her eyes off to the side she mulled over where the conversation was going. Snapping her gaze back to him she voiced her opinion, "Can we not talk about work?"

"Oh. Uh…sure." His eyes shifted as he filed through his thoughts. "What should we talk about?"

"What about this date? You know, our agreement?"

"Oh. Right." Ben paused for a moment before clearing his throat. He couldn't quite bring himself to look into Mari's eyes and hold a conversation at the same time. She had her hair halfway up and the rest tumbled down her back and over her nude shoulders. The dress she wore was an eyelet fabric in a soft sage green that complemented her skin tone. "Uh…y-you look very n-nice, Mari."

Mari couldn't help the immediate flush to her cheeks. She hadn't expected him to compliment her right out of the gate. Elation simmered deep with her to hear the words from his mouth. Even if he was pretending for the sake of their experiment.

"Oh well…thank you. You know…you can look at me, Ben." She paused as she shifted in her seat. "Actually, you should always look at your date." Timidly his gaze raised to meet hers and she could see the obvious and immediate fluster. Mari laughed as she leaned her elbows onto the table and propped her chin in her hands. "Remember…it's only me. I'm not going to run away screaming."

Ben should have been able to relax at her reassurance. Instead, the mere fact that it was a woman, one he had a growing attraction to who said it, made it even worse. But Mari was right. In order for this to work, they had to provide each other with helpful pointers and suggestions. No matter how awkward it might be, it was to get them through their dating slump.

"Ah…right." Taking a moment, Ben did his best to attempt to send his body into a more relaxed stance. He shouldn't be so stressed out. He had to treat this like a continuing education class. To study the moment and take notes before applying what he learned. "So…is what I selected to wear, is it acceptable?"

Mari leaned back in her seat with a laugh. A brow cocked on her forehead as she gave him a more exaggerated once-over.

"Lose the vest. Seriously. It's…a bit much. You could always add a few solid colors of dress shirts to your wardrobe. Simplify yourself. But …you didn't do too bad."

"Duly noted." Another long draw of silence was threatening their bordering-on-normal conversation. The two of them were so used to their solidarity, especially at meal times.

"So, what do you normally do when you meet a woman for dinner?" Mari's curiosity had gotten the better of her. She had an idea of what she liked on dates, but she was wondering what Ben considered to be acceptable.

"Well…I…um… I would pay for the bill." Ben offered, unsure if that was the correct answer.

"No, well, I mean that's nice of you and all, but I was talking about beforehand. Do you pick her up? Do you bring her flowers? What do you do?"

"Um…" Ben was at a loss for words. "I suppose what we did tonight. I meet her at the restaurant."

"Oh."

"Is that wrong?"

"Well…no, not exactly I guess." Mari paused. "I suppose its fine, especially if you talked it over before your date. Flowers are nice. Well, at least I like them." Ben filed that tidbit away for later. Even if all else failed, he could at least give Mari one decent date at the end of their trial. "Body language is big too."

"Body language?" Ben knew what she meant but he didn't realize that it could be such a big part of the courtship process.

"I literally write about it all day." Mari chuckled with a toss of her hair back over her shoulder. "How you hold yourself speaks volumes. It's a show, don't tell sort of thing. For example..." She draped her crossed arms over the edge of the table and leaned in closer to him. Her eyes moved to catch his curious gaze and a soft smile curled at her lips. "See? This shows that I'm interested in what you have to say."

Ben tried to blink away the heat in his cheeks as he shifted in his seat.

"You, on the other hand, look like you're ready to bolt for the fire exit." Mari cracked a grin in amusement. "Seriously, Ben. Relax. Take a deep breath. Relax your shoulders, maybe even lean on the table a bit." Closing his eyes, Ben did as Mari instructed. He took a few deep breaths and let his shoulders droop. Dropping his hands into his lap, he did feel a little more at ease. "There, see? Now you actually look like you don't mind being here with me."

An unexpected smile brightened his face with her encouragement and Mari felt her ears grow hot. The only smiles she had seen of his were quick and fleeting, hardly a smile at all. This one, this one seemed genuine. Now if only he could manage to smile like that all the time. Or maybe not. It left Mari completely disarmed. More so than one should be with something as simple as a smile.

"Oh…wow…a smile too. Uh…very nice." Her voice warbled a bit as she tried to clear her throat.

"Smiles are good, yes?"

"Very good. Yes. Yeah." Mari nodded enthusiastically, avoiding his gaze. She was grateful for the sudden reappearance of the waiter with their drinks. Anything to distract her from saying or doing something stupid. Their budding conversation had to regrettably pause. They placed their dinner order with the waiter who was giving them a cautious side-eye. Even he could sense that this was a first date that was not going very well.

"So."

"So."

They needed to get away from the prolonged uncomfortable silences. Neither of them liked making small talk. Mari for one would rather have teeth pulled instead of talking with a random person at the grocery store.

"Shit." Mari spat out which shocked Ben with her abrupt curse. "Maybe we need like…flashcards or something. Or a list of questions? Is that a thing?"

"Oh…I don't know. I mean…perhaps?" Ben couldn't help but smirk to himself. "Do you need an alcoholic drink?"

Mari immediately balked at the suggestion. It was going to be a long time before she ever drank that much again.

"That was a joke, wasn't it?"

"A little tease."

"I'm never going to live that night down, am I?"

Ben shook his head with a laugh. There was that laugh again. That glorious warm and honeyed laughter that seemed to always make her breath catch.

"I do not think so."

"Dammit."

Once their food arrived, the two ceased all conversation. Their hunger went to the forefront. The food was delicious. It was difficult to pull away for even a sliver of dialog. Mari was halfway through her plate when she realized that she hadn't spoken a word to Ben in quite some time.

"I think dinner was a bad idea."

Immediately Ben lifted his gaze to hers and there was a tinge of fear. "...What?"

"Dinner. It's nothing but small talk."

"Oh."

"We suck at small talk."

"True."

"We should go do something fun. Like…an activity or something." Mari offered as she glanced over at Ben. She swung her fork around midair for emphasis. "Something where we don't have to stare at each other and can distract ourselves with other things."

The suggestion was not meant to be suggestive, but Ben almost choked on a brussle sprout. Mari raised a brow at him, and he gave her a reassuring half smile that he was okay. Doing something off the wall, albeit a bit goofy, might do them some good. To take the stress off of trying to keep a conversation flowing.

"Like mini golf?" Ben suggested after clearing his throat and wiping his mouth on a napkin. With a subtle tilt of her head, Mari pondered his idea.

"Actually…not half-bad, McGregor. Do you think you could let loose to play mini golf?"

"I suppose you'll have to see." A smile quirked at the corner of his mouth.

Chapter Ten

Friday morning burned bright and early. Mari dragged herself down to the bakery. The night before with Ben had not been late, but she found herself in a struggle to get out of bed. She had to down her coffee in record time. However, now she was going to have to spend the rest of the day nursing a burnt tongue as she had no patience to wait for it to cool.

"Well, good morning to you too." Shannon popped up from behind the counter as Mari made her way into the main part of the shop. She grabbed her apron off the wall hook in a huff, praying for the coffee to kick in and give her the jump-start she needed.

"Yeah yeah…" Mari dismissed her as she shuffled into the back. She reappeared with a tray of freshly baked cream-filled donuts. Shoving one into her mouth, she maneuvered her way back to the glass display cases to slide the tray inside.

"Hey! No sampling of the merchandise!" Shannon teased as she shot Mari a look.

"Consider it my tip."

"You didn't even serve any customers!"

"A preemptive tip?"

The cream-filled donuts were heaven on earth and Mari's eyes rolled back as she partook. It was worth the tease from Shannon, even though she knew her friend didn't mind. It's not like she was devouring a whole tray. Except perhaps if it was a stressful day then she might accomplish such a feat.

"I hope you are enjoying my cream!" Luke shouted from the kitchen. The two women looked at each other and erupted in snorting laughter. The filling almost shot straight out Mari's nose before she managed to swallow her bite mid-laugh.

"You gave me quite the mouthful!" Mari yelled back, and she thought that Shannon was going to pass out from laughing so hard. Despite her lack of an active sex life, Mari could dish out the "that's what she said" jokes without hesitation.

"Alright, alright. We have to keep it at least PG now." Shannon warned the both of them as she wiped the tears from her eyes. "I'm unlocking the front door."

The morning passed by in a blur. As usual, the bakery had a line out the door and down the street at opening time. Mari's caffeine kicked in just in time. It helped her fulfill customers' orders with ease. One after another she sent them on their merry way to enjoy their treats from Kohler's.

"Just think, Mari. This is your last weekend doing it solo. The hired help starts up in a week." Shannon reminded Mari as she had a free moment to pull the empty trays from their cases. Letting out a sigh, Mari leaned against the counter to take the weight off her aching feet. It was past 12 pm which meant only a few stragglers would be in and out.

The antique bell on the door rang, announcing another customer. Mari adjusted her position and looked up to see Ben staring back at her. She felt frozen for a moment. His gaze was no longer looking upon her in morbid fascination, as it had so many times before. The look in his intriguing blue eyes had softened. Almost as if there was some sort of delight to see her.

"Ben! A little late today. Your order is all ready to go." Shannon's voice broke the unknown tension in the air. Ben moved his attention to Shannon as she held out his order. Blinking, Mari tried to get her thoughts together. Shannon shot her a curious look. Blindsided by the appreciative nod Ben offered, he shocked Shannon with a smile too.

"Thank you again." Shannon's jaw dropped in surprise, and she watched him turn to leave. But not before he looked over to Mari with a warmer smile. "Goodbye, Mari."

All Mari could do was nod in astonishment. Ben must have been working on his mannerisms after all the notes Mari had given from the night before. It made her heart flutter as she watched him leave the bakery. Her eyes remained fixed on the door as she sat lost in thought.

"What. The fuck. Was that?" With a sharp emphasis on almost every word, Shannon stalked her way over to Mari. "That's the most I've ever heard him talk. How the fuck are you and Ben on a first-name basis?"

Mari shrugged her shoulders sheepishly. Turning, she busied herself with clearing out more of the empty trays. She wanted to avoid Shannon's questioning gaze as long as possible. The last thing she wanted was to tell her friend about her embarrassing agreement with Ben. How was she going to explain, in her desperation to write her book, that she recruited the help of the beyond-awkward librarian?

"Mari. Come on. I know you've got something juicy you're holding onto. Dish it, girl."

"It's…nothing."

Shannon followed Mari as she walked into the kitchen to put the trays on the growing stack. She could almost feel her friend breathing down her neck in her pursuit. Her intense stare fixated on the back of Mari's head. It made her skin prickle with Shannon's unrelenting nosiness.

"Come on. Out with it. I'm not going to leave you alone until you do."

Mari cast a glance at Luke who had his earbuds in, bobbing his head to some unknown beat. He was busy scrubbing the pile of prep bowls from earlier in the morning. With a heavy sag of her shoulders and a sigh to match, Mari turned back to her friend. She could not meet her gaze and instead stared at her sneakered feet.

"It's…it's just a little…experiment."

"Experiment?! Hold up… What the fuck are you doing in your spare time? You're supposed to be writing."

"I am writing! Or well…trying to." Mari scraped the palms of her hands down her face in her exasperation. "Look I was desperate and I-"

"Whoa whoa whoa whoa. Girl. You're barely here a month and already getting some ass! Although your choice in man is not exactly who I-"

"Oh my god, Shannon. *NO.*" Mari stared at her friend, a bit mortified that Shannon assumed that Mari and Ben had slept together. The idea hadn't exactly avoided her thoughts, but how desperate did she seem? "Look. My publisher is breathing down my neck because they want a new book, and they want a new book with more…*spice*. Romance. All the shit I know *nothing* about. I've been stressing for months about how the hell I'm going to write this fucking book. And then Ben goes ahead and offers the idea of us…*experimentally dating*. Dating to see what it's like. To figure out what we are doing wrong in relationships and figuring out how to fix it. It's just…research."

Shannon looked as if her eyes were going to fall out of her head. Mari had unloaded months of stress on her friend and spilled the beans on her awkward pet project.

"So that's why you've been avoiding me after work? You've been so hung up on your book?"

"Partly." Mari shrugged and looked down in shame. There was a moment of pause before Shannon enveloped her friend in her arms.

"Mari, you are amazing and a gifted writer. You shouldn't be so hard on yourself." Shannon pulled back with a tease of a smile. "Even if your search history and research are beyond questionable. We will hide the bodies together, remember?"

Tilting her head back with a laugh, Mari relaxed and nodded.

"Yeah, yeah."

"So…you and Ben huh?"

"Shut up."

Chapter Eleven

Mini golf that following Monday was treating the two of them far better than the awkward dinner. It was apparent to Mari that Ben had taken her feedback to heart. He was less quiet and seemed more at ease around her. Instead of being stuck at a table during dinner and staring at each other, the distraction with the activity at hand helped the flow of their conversation.

Their technically third date started with awkward silence yet again, but Ben warmed up in the sport of competition. They were a few holes in on the pirate-themed 18-hole course of a tourist trap. Mari was already beating Ben handily. He had restored to teasing her before he egged her on and tried to dissuade her from her streak.

"If I didn't know better, I'd say you were trying to throw me off my game." Mari chided as she sunk another putt for par. Ben heard the clunk of the ball and groaned. He begrudgingly stepped up to his blue golf ball that was unfortunately quite a few feet away from the hole.

Mari had almost laughed out loud when Ben showed up in khaki cargo shorts and a college shirt. She wasn't even sure if his legs had ever seen the sun with how pale they were. He insisted it was his overseas heritage, but Mari chided right back that he was some sort of book vampire. The playful back and forth helped eased Ben into more of a relaxed state.

"I would do no such thing." Ben defended, as innocently as possible as he stepped up to his ball and eyed up his shot. He glanced up at her. The look took her by surprise. Mari blushed and moved her gaze away from his, pretending to study her ball.

Smiling to himself, he shifted his sandaled feet and lined up his golf club with the ball to aim his shot. She had dressed down to something more comfortable for the warm but breezy evening. Despite the simplicity of her t-shirt and linen shorts, they rode high on her thigh. Ben couldn't help but let his eyes drift up the swath of naked skin.

Unable to move his eyes away, he missed his putt and cursed under his breath. He watched it sail right past the hole.

"Oooh…not even close, McGregor."

"Hush you." He shot right back at her taunt. He was going to have to pull himself together if he was going to at least try to beat Mari. She was good. Very good. Better than one should be at mini golf. Ben took two more shots before he finally sunk his ball into the hole. Mari gave him a snide round of applause and he stuck his tongue out at her. Her laugh was bright and sweet. Ben felt warm and tingly upon hearing it.

Mari stepped up to the next hole. She took a moment to figure out the proper ball placement to get around the obstacles in her way. She was methodical in her reasoning. Ben admired the way she took her time to plot a strategy. The way her body moved, bent, and twisted intrigued him. It was almost as if it was how her mind processed things when she worked on writing her best-selling novels.

Always looking to the goal but cautious of the journey to the end.

"Ben?" He blinked as he finally realized that Mari had been saying his name. "Is my underwear showing or something?" Ben blushed and shifted. He began to sweat with her odd question.

"Ah...n-no, why?"

"Is it something else?"

Of course, it was, but Ben would not admit it.

"No, no. You're fine."

"You keep staring at me. It's only making me a bit paranoid." There was an immediate blush that bloomed on the apples of his cheeks and along the line of his auburn beard. He needed to be more subtle about this.

"I-uh...um..." He stuttered, trying to figure out what to say. "Well...didn't you t-tell me that I should look at my date?"

"Oh." It was now Mari's turn to blush as she looked away and back down at her golf ball. "Right. I did. Um...good job." How the hell was she going to accomplish anything if she had that heated prickle along her spine whenever she felt his gaze? He needed to look at her, engage her in conversation, touch her, tease her... But one thing at a time. He had the adoring look perfected. If her body had anything to say about the matter.

Taking a deep breath, she took her shot. She was off her game and her ball rolled short of the hole.

"Hmm...looks like I might finally have a chance," Ben jested as he stepped up to the tee. Lining up his shot, he gave the ball a good wack. It whizzed right past the hole to ricochet off the back wall and almost took her golf ball out in the process.

"You were saying?" She looked up from the settling place of their two balls with a smug grin.

"Yeah, yeah. That was only one stroke."

"Oh well, then, by all means, show me up."

Mari stepped up to her ball and did her best to even her breathing and align her putt. There were only a few holes left. If she continued to mess up like that then Ben maybe had a chance of winning. It seemed to her that he had a thirst for competitiveness to him.

As she was pulling back in her swing, there was an abrupt outburst from Ben that startled her.

"What do you think about sex?"

The overwhelming fluster washed over her and ruined her follow through. She hit the ball too hard and sent it flying through the air. It whizzed past a startled Ben. He ducked and the ball dropped into the nearby water hazard with an obnoxious plop.

"I-I'm sorry. *What?*" Mari stuttered out after she got over the initial shock of the question and her terrible shot.

"You know…sex. I-Is that not something one does when dating?"

Her eyes stared at him with some sort of muted incredulousness. She didn't know how to respond to the question that seemed to have come from out of the blue.

"W-Well…I-I mean…yes…"

"So…is that not something that…w-we should do as well?"

Mari was at a loss for words. The flush that went through her body overheated her so much that she felt as if she was going to swoon. She planted her golf club down onto the green to keep her steady.

"I…I…uh…its… Perhaps." She turned away him slipped past to retrieve her ball. The last thing she wanted to do was elaborate on that subject matter any further, and in public no less. It wasn't as if she hadn't thought about it. The thought had crossed her mind. On more than one occasion. She had tried her best to suppress it, to sweep the thoughts under the rug as they weren't necessary.

She grabbed the ball retrieval tool with determination. Although it was more of an eagerness to get the unwieldy thoughts out of her head. Which made the attempt to retrieve her ball go rather poorly. Her mind could not concentrate on the task at hand. It kept repeating his question over and over again in her head. What would it be like to have sex with Ben? Would it be as awkward as his conversations?

"Here." Ben reached out and covered her hands with his to assist her. His tenderness startled her along with the sudden rush of heat that radiated out from his touch. "Let me help." His voice was soft by her ear. He helped maneuver her arms to better use the ball retrieval tool to scoop her ball from the vibrant blue water.

"Oh…uh…t-thanks…" Was all that Mari could utter as Ben helped her dump the sodden ball back onto the green. This was the closest he had been to her since helping her to bed. Except this time, she was conscious and completely sober. His touch lingered longer than necessary but he did not pull away.

Mari felt it. That draw. As much as she wanted to give in, it terrified her. She severed the connection abruptly as she pulled away to put the ball retriever back.

"Y-You're welcome." He added softly as he picked up his club to return to their game. His question had left her discombobulated. She managed to bogie on the hole. If his goal was to throw her off of her game, then he had accomplished that.

It was true that Ben had initially used the question to distract Mari. It was a dirty trick, but he had tried to attempt some semblance of humor. After she had called him out on it, he was more careful in his watch of her. She was much quieter than she had been in the earlier part of the evening which caused Ben to grow more concerned.

"We should go get ice cream."

Her suggestion came out of nowhere after he sank his putt. Even with the awkwardness, Mari didn't want to end their evening quite yet. Trying to keep his smile to himself, Ben nodded as Mari teed up for the next hole.

"That sounds good."

Mari was still feeling heated as she stood off to the side after her turn. She watched Ben make his final few putts. Even with the water hazard embarrassment, she still easily won. The evening had proved to be rather fun, even with Ben's inelegant inquiry.

"Shall we?" Ben offered his arm to Mari after they returned their clubs. Her eyes moved to his extended elbow, and she felt the heat rise back up to her cheeks. The unexpected offer of his arm required a close sort of intimacy that Mari wasn't sure Ben could handle.

"Let's go get ice cream." Her voice was a bit gravelly as she curled her palm around the crook of his elbow. A soft smile crept up to the corner of her mouth. It was a rather polite and chivalrous move on his part and Mari felt herself melt a bit with the gesture.

It was a bit awkward at first. But within a few steps down the concrete sidewalk, the two of them eased into the closeness and relaxed. Their biceps brushed every so often. More so when they needed to steer clear of the families walking opposite of them. The near-constant bumping against each other made Mari thankful that they headed for a cold treat.

"You paid for golf, let me get the ice cream." Mari offered when she was finally able to find her voice.

Ben glanced down at her with a cocked brow and chuckled.

"That is a fair compromise."

"Well…relationships are all about compromise. And negotiations." She teased with a laugh.

"Honest communication in a relationship is key, is it not?"

Mari looked up at him in wonder. Of course, he was correct. It was unusual for a man to bring that essential, and usually forgotten, rule to the forefront. Ben remembered that it was an important aspect of relationships. But his near-constant anxiety often made it difficult for him to voice his feelings.

"You're right. It is." If they were both going to learn how to be a proper partner, then they needed to talk about everything. Including the more intimate parts, however uncomfortable it might be. "I believe we had a decent go at communication tonight, don't you think?"

"Indeed. I have…found that speaking to you is well…becoming easier each day that we see each other."

"Ah, so the secret to cracking Ben McGregor is making him submit to exposure therapy."

A burst of laughter sounded from his mouth as he tossed his head back with his mirth. Mari brushed off her lopsided and wilting smile before he caught her gaze once again.

"Yes, I suppose that is true. My anxiety thanks you."

"Mine thanks you as well."

The two erupted into more laughter as they walked into the ice cream shop. After some deep thought over the menu choices, they placed their orders. Sundae Best offered some of the more unusual, yet delicious, flavors on the island. They always changed from season to season. Mari tried to make a stop there every year but sometimes it wasn't always feasible. Being two blocks down from the mini golf place made tonight the perfect excuse to visit.

The vintage doorbell in the ice cream shop chimed its cheery farewell as the two wandered back out onto the street. There was a more sizable line outside of the popular ice cream shop as the warm evening tumbled into dusk. Both of them ordered the small waffle cone, which was much larger than either had expected. They shared in a feisty battle against the warm night air melting their ice cream.

"Would you like to walk down to Surfside Park?" Ben offered as he dipped his head down for another long lick of his gingersnap ice cream. Mari stood there transfixed. She stared at the broad swath of his tongue as it methodically caressed the drips away from the edge of his cone.

"Huh?" she uttered in a daze as her own cone of key lime pie was already dribbling down and over the heft of her thumb. Normally, she would have been swift to tend to the wayward trickles before they reached her skin. Instead, the artful way that Ben's tongue smoothed the melting heft of ice cream held her rapt attention.

"The park? Would you like to walk there?" he asked again with a cocked brow and paused his licking. It was only then that Mari blinked her way back to the present and noticed the dripping ice cream.

"Oh shit. I mean, yes. Yes, I would. Just give me a second to get this nuclear meltdown under control." Ben laughed but his mirth faded as he watched her mouth descend to ward off the melting exterior of her scoop. Her pink lips opened wide as she inelegantly slurped up the dripping concoction. She added in her lapping tongue to pick up all the rouge drops.

Ben felt his throat go dry as his gaze widened at her innocent enjoyment of her ice cream cone. Her tongue was graceful and adept in its work. She had her meltdown under control in no time at all. Unfortunately, there was something in his shorts that had become a bit out of control.

Cleaning his throat, he shifted his body to avoid her gaze. He pretended to tend to wipe some unseen drips of ice cream on his shirt. It was a vain attempt to quiet his racing heart and aching body. Mari was still distracted with devouring her ice cream that she didn't notice his *growing* issue.

Letting out a quick breath, Ben felt that he was calm enough to turn back around to her. He offered her a napkin. With a bit of laughter, she took it and wiped the saliva off her hand from where she had tried to rid her skin of the sticky ice cream. With their cones now well in order, the pair continued on their way down towards the park by the beach.

Chapter Twelve

It was a breezy night and cloudless, but not chilly. The sea air was a welcome relief against the mild humidity that was still rampant. The mugginess eased with each house they passed as they walked closer to the beach. They walked in silence, devouring their ice cream before any more of a mess came to be.

Mari had begun to notice that there was a growing ease with the quiet between them. Like some sort of unspoken language where their bodies seemed to fall into the same comfortable rhythm. But that was not the goal of their exercise. The goal was for both of them to become more comfortable with the experiences of dating and romance. Even if they were fake.

"Moonlit walks on the beach are very romantic, you know," Mari stated as she crunched down the rest of her waffle cone. "You're lucky. You live right by the beach so you could literally take all your dates on one."

"But…what if they have an aversion to sand? Or just…don't like it? It's so coarse and it gets everywhere."

"Come on, Ben. Just work with me." Mari pleaded with an exasperated laugh. "Most women would love it."

Ben had finished his cone a few houses back, but he could still taste the sharp ginger on his tongue. He cast her a questioning look but felt that he knew the answer. It seemed that she was attempting to subtly allude to something she liked.

The pair walked up and onto the boardwalk that radiated out from the small, covered pavilion. From their vantage point, they could almost make out the white of the cresting waves beyond the sand dunes.

"Do you enjoy long walks on the beach? Especially in the moonlight?"

"I love them."

"Well then. By all means, we must promenade." Ben said it with such a proper gusto to his English accent that made it seem that he was a lord from the Regency period. Mari couldn't help but giggle.

"I don't think I could have said it better myself."

"Shall we?" Ben bent his arm at the elbow and offered it back to her. Mari took his lead without the slightest bit of hesitation this time. The pair made their way down the ramp of pebbled sand through the sand dunes to the beach. When they reached the looser sand, she kicked off her flip-flops and picked them up.

Mari wasn't exactly a fan of the sand. But the cathartic feeling of her bare feet sinking into the chilly softness never ceased to calm her. The sand was cool as they meandered their way down to the shoreline. The roar of the ocean waves drowned out most of their inner thoughts and the two were thankful for the reprieve.

"Even with the wild and unbridled churn of the ocean, it does nothing but bring me peace."

"That's very lovely." Ben looked down at her with a softened gaze. Mari glanced up at him with a smile. "Yet again, you've always had a lyrical way with words. It's no wonder myself and others are fans of your work." The smile turned into a red flush on her cheeks, and she averted her gaze.

"Does the sea bring you peace?" She added, not addressing his compliment. His eyes turned back out to the horizon that had long since blended with the inky black color of the sky.

"It does. Perhaps not in the same way it pertains to you. But…I do enjoy my time by the ocean."

"What else do you like to do, Ben? What calms or comforts you?"

Her unique question hit Ben unexpectedly. It was one of the more profound ones that she had asked since their little experiment had started. The kind of questions that help a person get to know someone's soul.

"Well…I suppose a good cup of loose-leaf tea. Obviously, books. Hardbacks are my favorite. Classical music. A good scone." He turned to look at her with a smile that quirked at the corner of his mouth. It made his auburn beard twitch. "I am a very boring person, aren't I?" Mari shook her head with a laugh. Her hand, still enveloped in the crook of his elbow, offered a reassuring caress against his bicep.

"Not at all. Maybe a bit more…*distinguished* than your average person. But…well, that's what makes you…so interesting." Mari didn't want to say anything fake. What she offered was the truth.

"I-I don't think anyone has ever called me 'interesting' before."

"Well…you are," she added quickly as they continued along the beach.

Ben cleared his throat as the quiet settled back between them again.

"If the ocean brings you such calm, why do you not live here?"

"Ben, are you asking me to move in? I think the second date is a bit too soon to bring that up." She could feel him tense but then relax as he realized that she had been joking. Despite her trying her best to keep a straight face, Mari erupted into laughter.

"Oh…ah, yes. Right." With a strained laugh, he nodded his head in agreement. "But why don't you live here? It seems like your stressors with your career might…subside a bit."

"You aren't wrong. It's just…I don't know. I have comfort in my home. I can afford more space back home. Here I might be able to only manage an apartment or condo. That is if I'm lucky." A heavy sigh sagged her shoulders. "But yes. One day I would like to. Perhaps after another successful bestseller…or two."

The two continued their leisurely stroll for a bit before Ben broke the silence.

"I have a question." Mari glanced up at him, curious. "So…for example. If I was a prospective suitor…I should say something along the lines that 'I am enjoying your presence'. Correct?" Mari nodded with encouragement. Although to her it sounded as if Ben was doing his best to avoid an admission of something personal. Instead, he twisted it into a learning exercise. "It would be nice for you to visit the library for longer than only the summer," Ben added quietly. He looked down at his feet, kicking up the sand as they walked.

Mari swallowed dryly but rebounded without hesitation. "I thought you were annoyed and exasperated with me leeching off the Wi-Fi?"

"Perhaps a bit..." Ben admitted with a quiet chuckle. "But I have been enjoying you using the library as your private office."

"That still makes it sound as if you're annoyed with me." She teased as his laughter warmed and continued.

"I do believe I am on the right track then. Aren't most couples annoyed with each other?" Now it was Mari's turn to outright laugh. His abrupt attempt at humor had taken her by surprise. It took her a moment to get her laughter under control.

"That's true. But usually not around the second date. The loving annoyance comes much, much later. From what I've seen anyway. It sounds awful but, I don't know, the mutual loving annoyance seems very much in my wheelhouse." Her eyes moved up to his face as a smile softened her lips. "I'm surprised you haven't been in a lasting relationship. You're really good at being annoying. Although...maybe you haven't been able to keep it hidden for long enough to trap them." Mari was humoring herself at this point with her playful jabs.

"Maybe I only want to annoy you." It was meant to only be a tease, but the husky drop and slow cadence of his voice led her to believe otherwise. Ben eased the pair to a stop and turned to look down upon Mari who had tilted her chin up in question. With a purse of her lips, a languid smile made its way across the swath.

The chill in the air had vacated the encroaching space between them. His heart fluttered as he watched her smile. Despite the breezy evening, he could make out the scent of her perfume. It was soft and floral. Jasmine, perhaps? Whatever it was, it was intoxicating, and he felt himself leaning in closer.

"Are you trying to kiss me, Ben?" Her sudden whisper stopped him cold, and his eyes flashed open. He didn't realize that his body decided to go on autopilot. The flutter of her racing heart had almost made her choke on her words.

"I..."

"Uh...I-I mean..." Why did she have to open her big mouth? Her anxiety had gotten the better of her. Instead of closing her eyes and enjoying the moment she had to go and ruin it. Her gaze moved to study his lips as he continued to stand there, frozen and hovering above her. "I-It's something that um...does happen when dating. So...I mean...we should at least try it..." Mari's words came out disjointed while distracted by how plump his lips looked.

Ben's eyes widened in surprise. A woman just told him that he could kiss her. There was no way that he was going to miss an opportunity like that. Especially not with Mari. She had enchanted him all evening with her playful and sometimes unintended humor.

"Yes...we should...try."

Time seemed to stand still. The ocean had grown quiet as the roar of blood rushed through his ears was almost deafening. The moment seemed almost otherworldly. The soft breeze wafted through, as the moonlight danced across the gentle waves. He raised a trembling hand and brushed his fingers over the enticing plumpness of her cheek.

Mari felt her eyelids grow heavy. How was this disconcerting and nerdy-as-hell man bringing her to a point where she could no longer resist? His touch was almost electric on her skin as she leaned into the caress. Was it the odd awkwardness between them that added to the unusual intrigue?

It was then that their lips timidly met. They managed to attach a bit off-center but neither of them minded. Ben's touch became firmer, surer after a long moment of the initial touchdown. The feeling was… *peculiar*. Something neither of them could put their finger on. Something neither of them had ever quite felt before. Something neither of them ever wanted to forget.

The swirl of emotions was turbulent low in her stomach as his fingers dipped back into her hairline. There was such a heated build-up in only a few moments, and it had left her breathless. Something about this kiss was unusual.

Until it hit her. Hard and sudden as an unexpected strike of lightning. She was actually feeling *something*. Mari was feeling *everything*. Everywhere. All at once. There was some sort of emotion in their connection. A heated and confusing jumble of feelings that were lighting a fire.

Mari broke their embrace abruptly with a sharp gasp and an open-mouthed grin.

Finally.

Inspiration hit her hard with their experimental kiss. Their daft plan was finally working.

Ben had been so enveloped in their kiss that with the abrupt loss of her body to prop him up, he felt himself stumble. But it wasn't a subtle shift in his body weight. It was a full-blown face plant into the sand next to her as his weakened knees gave out from under him.

A sharp squeak of surprise escaped her as she jumped back with her hands covering her mouth. There was a moment of outrageous concern before she realized that the man might have very well fainted from the kiss. The comical puff of sand that shot out from around his body made Mari erupt in laughter.

"Oh god, Ben! I'm sorry!"

Kneeling down, she reached out to grab onto his arm to help him up. As soon as Ben's face rose back up from the sand, he was already mid-laugh. The embarrassment might have killed him with anyone else. But with Mari, he didn't have to worry. Well except for the random incessant teases from now on for being such a bumbling buffoon.

"I'm fine. I'm fine." Ben slowly rose to sit back on his knees as he attempted to sputter out the sand from his mouth. There was desperation to be rid of the dreadful sand on his hands and glasses on a clean part of his shorts. Cautiously he used his hands to brush the sand from his face, but it was a slow and arduous task.

Feeling rather guilty of the face that he was in this predicament because of her, Mari stepped up to him and assisted with her clean hands. The wet sand was persistent as it remained on his skin and stuck in his beard.

"Hold on, let me. Close your eyes." Shoving her hand into the hemline of her shirt, she managed to wrap the fabric around her palm. Using the inelegant but helpful tool, Mari was able to rid most of the sand from his face. Being discombobulated from the kiss and his sand bath, he felt a bit woozy. He opened his eyes to focus on something to stop the world from spinning.

The sight of Mari's bare navel almost sent him careening backward. Immediately heat rose to his already-flushed cheeks. He was thankful for the dim light of the moon to hide their flustered color. She was so gentle in her touch, taking her time to remove the granules of sand away from his eyes and mouth. If he hadn't already maxed out his limit on courage, he would have leaned forward to kiss the dip in her abdomen.

"Uh…t-thanks…"

"Hell no, Ben. I should be thanking you!" Her shirt lowered and a flourish of sand fell out as she cut off the visual that captivated Ben's attention. His brow furrowed in confusion as he eased himself back up to his feet with her help.

"Me?"

"I know what I'm doing with my book!" Mari let out an excited squeal as she jumped around in the sand. "I know the library is closed but I need to get these ideas down as soon as possible. Even if I have to write them down on paper! I hope you don't mind if I run to go work on it, do you?"

Ben had to grit his teeth to stop his facial expression from falling into disappointment. The evening had been a dream. Even with the random moments of embarrassment. It had gone much better than their uncomfortable dinner from the week before. As much as he didn't want her to leave, her finding inspiration for writing her book had always been the top priority.

"Oh uh…sure. By all means. Go ahead." Ben forced a smile and a nod. Mari grabbed him by his biceps as she leaned in to press a quick yet firm kiss on his cheek with a jovial grin.

"Thank you! You're the best!" As she darted towards the nearest beach access, Ben turned to watch. She had ended the date by running away but kept her promise as it was not from him specifically. She was running towards her career and livelihood. For now, Ben considered it to be a tick in the dating win column. Now the question was, would she come back?

Chapter Thirteen

Mari had gone through half a notebook's worth of paper of scribbled notes and timelines. A whole slew of information was spewed across the pages. The words were pouring out and her hand could barely keep up with the output. Giving her eyes a rest, she looked up to see the soft orange hue of sunrise coming in through the window. The break in her writer's block had taken the entire night.

The bakery was closed and she was thankful for not needing to rush downstairs. She felt the crushing weighted blanket of sleep attempting to smother her. With a yawn, she rose from her seat at the small kitchen table. Wandering over to the sink she deposited her coffee cup. It had been heavily used throughout the night. She was in desperate need of a shower and some fresh shots of espresso.

It was as good a spot as any to stop and move on to some much-needed self-care. Not to mention the sheer fact that she had noticed herself nodding off throughout the past hour. She needed to get up and walk around a bit to get the blood flowing. To wake herself up.

Grabbing her phone, she walked to her bathroom. She texted Shannon to see if she wanted to join her for coffee.

Mari knew she was up. Shannon tried to keep her sleep schedule close to the usual bakery's needs, even on the days the shop was closed. Shannon had been right. Mari had been neglecting one of the other reasons why she had been invited to stay in the apartment. To spend time with her friend all summer, beyond helping out in the shop.

She had been so consumed by the urge to keep her publisher and agent happy that she had neglected herself and her friend in the process. If Faith wanted her next bestseller, she was going to have to wait. Mari was now back to square one. Considering that she had completely scrapped the idea she had been working on for the past month. With the productive sleepless hours of the night, she had constructed a detailed timeline and wrote most of the first chapter of the book with her new idea.

As the hot water rained down on her body, her fingers drifted up to her lips. The kiss with Ben last night had unleashed something. Something unbridled and wild that sent all her senses into a tizzy. It was a feeling that she wanted to consume quickly and yet relish slowly all at the same time.

Where had a bumbling and shy man like Ben learned to kiss like that? It wasn't like he did anything different than the other men she had kissed. It just *felt* different. His mouth hit her lips like a jolt of electricity before it ran straight down to her toes. None of her previous kisses had ever come close to that one. They had been wet...and chaste. With no feeling behind them whatsoever.

Her phone buzzed on the sink with a text alert. With a head full of shampoo, she parted the curtain to sneak a peek at her screen. Shannon had enthusiastically agreed to the coffee date. Mari let loose a quick squeal of delight before diving back into her shower. She was beginning to feel more awake already. Although once her next caffeine fix wore off, she would be collapsing in bed for a long nap.

Fresh from her shower, she twisted her hair into a French braid and threw on a t-shirt and shorts as she scrambled out the door. Shannon was waiting for Mari at the foot of the steps to the apartment. There was an unexpected smile on her face as she stepped down onto the sidewalk to set off with Shannon.

"Don't tell me you had sex with Ben and that's why you're in a good mood."

Mari immediately balked and turned to her friend with a deer-in-the-headlights look.

"You and sex, I swear to god."

"Just because you've had shit partners doesn't mean it's shitty for everyone else. So? Did it happen?"

"What? No! For fucks sake drop it. It's never going to happen. We are just…pretending to date, remember?"

"Yeah huh, okay. So did you randomly hook up with a guy last night then?"

"Shannon, I did *NOT* have sex. Jeezus. I'm going to tell Luke that he needs to put out more." Her friend snorted with laughter as the two walked through the door into the coffee shop. They gave their orders to the barista before they wandered over to a table by the window.

"So, what does have you all chipper this morning? You seem more like your usual self."

"It's gone!"

"What is?"

"My writer's block!" Shannon sat back in her seat with a laugh and shook her head.

"Well…congrats then." She leaned onto the table to get a good look at Mari. "But…have you even slept?" Their order swiftly arrived at their table. Mari reached out and brought her cup to her lips. She greedily sipped her latte with a double shot of espresso. They had managed to make a little flourish with the creamer, but she barely noticed. She needed that jolt to her brain as soon as possible, lest she face-plant on the table from sheer exhaustion.

"Nope."

"Mari. You're insane." With a sigh, Shannon shook her head before diving into her breakfast sandwich.

"No. I'm brilliant."

"So, what fixed you?"

"I kissed Ben." The completely nonchalant way that Mari answered caused Shannon to choke on her sandwich. Even though she had teased Mari earlier, she had not expected that answer to come about in their conversation. Shannon dropped her sandwich to her plate in shock.

"You *WHAT*."

"Well…technically…it was a mutual thing."

"Technically? Mutual? Hold up. There is so much you are leaving out."

"It's not that difficult to understand. Kissing is just another part of dating, right? It had to be done."

Shannon stared at her friend. Mari was talking about kissing the town oddball like it was a business transaction.

"I…uh sure? Do you really think this whole thing is a good idea?" Shannon shot Mari a cautious look as she sipped her coffee. The last thing she wanted was for Mari to get hurt over something so wildly asinine. "What happens if Ben actually ends up liking you?"

Mari hadn't considered that. Actually, that aspect hadn't exactly been discussed between the two of them. She supposed that it was an unspoken agreement that their arrangement was only a learning experience. Nothing more.

"You're funny. There's no way Ben would like me. Or me like him."

"Yeah, but you kissed him!"

"For science! Jeez." Mari dismissively rolled her eyes as she took a long drawl from her coffee mug. Shannon eyed her friend carefully for a moment.

"Well, obviously this scientific kiss did something to you."

"Yeah, it got rid of my writer's block."

"Yeah okay. If you say so." The tone in Shannon's voice caused Mari to take pause. "It made you feel something, didn't it? Like a straight wildfire down your body?" Mari stared back at her friend as a pink tinge rose to her cheeks. "No one goes around grinning like that after a kiss unless they felt something."

"Well…sort of…"

"That's what a kiss is *supposed* to do, Mari."

"Oh. *Oh.*" The realization hit her all at once. "Fucking dammit." She clenched her eyes shut as she uneasily put her cup down on the table.

"You felt that shit down to your toes, didn't you?" Mari couldn't bear to look her friend in the eyes as she nodded. Shannon let out a sharp jolt of laughter as she clapped her hands together. "Hah! I knew it!"

"Well, shit. Now what do I do?" The stress was evident on Mari's face. Was this revelation going to fuck up their arrangement? She couldn't let that happen. Not when it was working so well by offering her fodder for her book.

"Sometimes I forget you're like a borderline virgin. Shit like that doesn't mean you're in love necessarily. It could mean that you want to jump his bones because he turns you on." Mari wrinkled her nose as she considered Shannon's observation. The last thing she wanted to consider Ben as was an object of sexual desire. "Look, whatever you're doing with him is obviously helping you write your book. And bringing you out of whatever shell you've been hiding in."

Chapter Fourteen

Mari hadn't been able to go back to the library and face Ben. Not after their kiss and what Shannon had said. She was doing her best to deal with the shoddy internet signal and write what she could. In the second or even later drafts she could always go back and research the finer aspects of her settings. Right now, she needed to get out every single word possible. As long as this streak was going to last, she was going to ride it out to the bitter end.

By the end of the week, she had managed to amass more than 20,000 words towards her goal, about one-quarter of her book. Faith hadn't exactly been thrilled with the idea that Mari scrapped her original project. But once she read the first few chapters of her new book, it completely changed her mind.

"Mari. Holy shit. This is like…lightyears better than the chapter you sent me last month. And…what's this? Three more chapters in my inbox? What the hell are you on? Meth? It's okay. You can admit it to me."

Mari nervously laughed into the phone as she shuffled through her papers spread out on the small kitchen table.

"Just…a change of scenery." There was no way she could ever explain to Faith the real reason for her sudden surge in inspiration.

"You mean the beach condo? Holy heck you should just move there! Especially if this book is going to turn out like I hope it will. I mean…your personality and prose are still prevalent but *oof*. That tease of a slow burn is starting up and I'm dying to read more."

When she had seen Faith's name pop up on her phone, she dreaded what would come next. The last few conversations with her agent had not been pleasant. Now with this new book idea being sprung on her all of a sudden, she had not been looking forward to hearing what Faith had to say.

Faith's excitement was a welcomed response. With a relieved sigh, Mari smiled. She had been so unsure about the abrupt change in the storyline. But Faith's words reassured her that she was heading in the right direction. Her heart was more in this story too, instead of pulling something out of her ass to appease the publishing industry.

"Phew…I'm glad. I'm really excited about this. I hope it pans out like I want it to. Like how everyone wants it to."

"You and me both. So, what, do you think you'll have a full manuscript by the end of the summer?"

Mari pursed her lips as she considered Faith's question. Sure, she was on a roll now, but what about a week from now? Would she be all dried up with no new ideas? What if the writer's block came back? What would she do then?

"Well…you know me. I can't make any promises…"

"Oh, come on, Mari. I can already tell this story has lit a fire under your ass. Now lie to me and say yes so I can sleep tonight."

Snorting in her sudden burst of laughter, Mari couldn't help but nod as she voiced her agreement.

"Fine. Yes. End of summer."

"Good. Now that that's out of the way…how are you? Find any hot beach hunks down at the shore?"

Ben wasn't exactly "beach hunk" material. So, she didn't feel like she would be lying to Faith if she said no. It would be best if she steered the line of questioning away from any potential love interests. However hunky, nerdy, or fictional they might be.

"Ah…no. I'm actually working in my friend's bakery for the summer."

"No shit! You doing actual customer service work. Hell, maybe it will loosen you up for your next book tour."

"Yeah well, I'm not making any promises. I still am not a fan of lots of people."

"But they're your adoring fans! Be thankful you don't have any off-putting stalkerish ones or else you might really become a full recluse."

"Well…true. But you know me, I can put on a brave face. Then I will go and hide for a week to recuperate from all the peopling I have to do."

"You're lucky you're talented and that I like you. Or else you'd be in quite a pickle with anyone else."

Mari laughed as she made a face.

"And that's why I try not to do anything to piss you off. So…you're stuck with awkward ol' me."

"Perfect. Because I'm going to make you a household name with this damn book. It really is something special, Mari."

The compliment made her heart swell and she smiled.

"I hope so. Because apparently, I need to buy a place at the beach to keep cranking out works like this one."

"Fucking right, you do! I'm going to be the best agent ever and make sure that you do. With plenty left over of course. And then you can invite me to stay there to celebrate." Mari could almost feel the wink Faith would be giving her had they been talking in person.

"Of course. Because after this project, I'm going to need a vacation from this vacation."

Chapter Fifteen

For some reason or another, Mari continued to avoid Ben. She had been lost in her seemingly endless stream of writing. Each day she stayed nose-down in her work, engrossed in her project.

As much as Ben wanted to approach her, he couldn't bring himself to do so. His eyes hadn't strayed far from her figure over the last few days. She sat hunched over the glow of her laptop with her large headphones on. Clearly, she didn't want to be bothered. Which he understood. For the majority of the time that she sat in the library, her fingers were rhythmically clacking along the keys. He delighted in the fact that the daft idea he had offered to her a few weeks ago was actually working out in her favor.

Their last date had been amazing. Maybe the best date he had ever been on. Even with his usual awkwardness jumbling the evening. And that kiss. The kiss had been unexpected but appreciated in every way possible. He had never experienced a kiss quite like that. It was so soft but thrilling. It had left his brain completely vacant of coherent thought. Much like how he felt when he attempted a conversation with an attractive woman. But this was in a good way.

He was sure to await her every day and offer a smile, a wave, or a tender greeting whenever she stopped by the library. It was the only interaction with her that he had of late. Aside from when he stopped by the bakery. Shannon had given Ben apologetic eyes on a few occasions. He wondered if Mari had shared with her their little agreement. No one could understand how their beneficial arrangement could work, but he and Mari did.

Almost a week had passed since their last date and Ben was getting antsy. Was their agreement over? Was a kiss all she needed? There were so many unanswered questions that he wanted to speak with Mari about. But he felt that he couldn't do so. At least not while she was on her writing streak. Even though he really wanted to.

"Ben." The abruptness of his name broke through his deep thought. Mari had seemingly appeared out of thin air by the front desk and it startled him. She was well past her usual arrival time and looked like she hadn't slept in a day or two. He was certain that she was still wearing her pajamas. It also seemed that she had also neglected to brush her hair after sleeping in a ponytail.

"Mari... I-It's nice to see-"

Mari cut him off, a wild desperation in her eyes. "We need another date." Ben felt his heart swell up. It was as if his prayers had been answered. But there was still his concern over her current state.

"O-Okay...s-sure."

"Oh, thank god." With a dramatic flop of her arms onto the counter, she dropped her head into the awkward pillow of her limbs. A sigh of relief was followed by some odd mix of a groan. "It's gone... it's all gone."

"What is…?" Ben asked as so many terrifying things started to swim through his head.

"My writing mojo!" Mari exclaimed as she tossed her head back with a frown. "I need more inspiration. Like…yesterday. I'm halfway done but now I have no idea how to end it!" She collapsed back down into her folded arms with a whine. Ben attempted to hush her as some of the patrons were curiously eying the two of them up.

"Well…so, what about tonight?" Ben offered, trying to think through some date ideas in a hurry. "A walk on the boardwalk? Wildwood?"

With that, Mari shot back up with a big smile. She brushed away the tears that were welling in her eyes. Taken aback at her sudden change in demeanor, he froze as she vaulted her petite self over the edge of the counter to press a quick kiss on his cheek. Ben felt himself blush hotly as she pulled back, still holding onto her broad smile.

"You are saving the day yet again!" With a little jump of excitement, she turned and headed for the door. As she pushed the door open, she paused and turned to him. "Pick me up at 7?" Ben could only nod with his mouth hung open wide in surprise as he watched her leave the building.

She had grown comfortable enough to invite him to pick her up at least. Now was his chance. With two dates and a multitude of information under his belt, he thought he could attempt to give Mari the date of her dreams.

* * *

Ben stood on the little covered balcony at Mari's apartment door. Blood roared through his ears. His heart would not stop beating out of his chest. On his way home from work, he had spent an exuberant amount of time at the florist. Just so he could pick out the right bouquet for

Mari. Roses had seemed like a safe bet, but he wanted to get something closer to her personality.

Swallowing back his anxiety, he timidly knocked. Mari must have been waiting for him as there was only a half second before the door wooshed open. It looked like she had at least taken a nap and showered in their time apart, but there was still a sort of crazed look in her eye. Although as soon as she enveloped the vision of Ben, her gaze softened considerably as she blinked back tears.

"Hi, Mari." The words came out breathlessly as he looked upon her with a lopsided smile. It was only a date to the boardwalk, but she had chosen a more eye-catching floral sundress. She had her hair tied back in a loose bun at the nape of her neck. There hadn't been a time yet where the sight of her hadn't made his heart do an odd flip.

"Oh, Ben…" She trailed off with a warble to her voice as her eyes drifted between his face and the flowers he presented. No man had ever brought her flowers before. She had always thought that it would be nice to at least have it happen once. But she had not prepared herself for it to affect her in such a way. He had selected a lovely array of hydrangeas, roses, and daisies in varying hues of purple and blue. "A-Are those for…me?"

"Oh right. Um, yes. I brought you flowers." He jumbled through his words as he stated the obvious. With a quick extension of his arm, he offered them to her. Followed by a crooked smile and a flush on his cheeks.

"Thank you! You're so…sweet. You learned something about me and actually implemented it." It wasn't the most romantic compliment, but he still felt his chest puff out from elation. He had done something right to make his date happy. Turning away, she moved to brush the tears from her eyes. "Come in for a second so I can put them in water."

With a nod, Ben stepped inside and closed the front door behind him. Mari had already busied herself over the sink as she trimmed the stems down with scissors. He took the time to admire her from behind. With her hair up he could drink in the creamy arch of her neck as it met with her bare shoulders. The straps of her dress were tied into neat bows that obstructed part of his vision.

He could feel the heat rise in his body and he turned away briskly to hush the sultry thoughts. There had to be a way to get the more sexual thoughts under control. He wasn't a teenager with raging hormones anymore. And yet…he hadn't met anyone quite like Mari before.

The hand upon his shoulder jolted him from his torrid thoughts and he turned to uneasily smile down at Mari.

"Ready to go?"

"Absolutely."

The ride to Wildwood started off in silence. Ben couldn't relax. Not with Mari sitting right next to him in his car and looking rather alluring. He had to keep himself as calm and collected as possible. There was no way he could afford to screw up another date with his bumbling nonsense. He wanted this one to go flawlessly. Third time's a charm, right?

"I can't believe you got me flowers." Her statement was abrupt and almost felt foreign as it broke the silence. Ben cast her a cautious look in question.

"Was I…not supposed to?"

Mari felt a flush on her cheeks as she hunched down a bit in her seat. "Oh no, you were. It was great. I'm…still in awe of it." She glanced at him with a playful look. "Just let me wallow in this moment."

Ben chuckled to himself with a nod. Her endless compliments from the simple gesture beefed up his ego in all the best ways. He was more than ready for this date.

Maybe he would even be brave enough to hold her hand. Perhaps even be ballsy enough to kiss her again.

After the two found a parking spot, they wandered up the entrance ramp to the Wildwood boardwalk. It was the start of peak season and a perfect night with low humidity. Families and teens were out in droves. Not exactly the ideal sort of social situation for either of them.

Mari froze at the top of the ramp. She was unsure of which direction to head. There was a desperate attempt to keep her cool with the throngs of noisy people passing them. Noting her apprehension, and feeling the same sort of thing himself, Ben shifted closer to her side. His eyes dropped to her heaving chest. With her increasing anxiety her bosom was moving up and down rapidly. Even though he was feeling it himself, he wanted to do what he could to comfort her.

Reaching down, his hand brushed against the outside of hers. It was a gentle coax before his fingers intertwined and locked with her digits. The touch snapped her out of her downward spiral, and she looked over at Ben. His hand clutched hers tightly and her face softened from his gesture of comfort. It did what he had intended. It distracted her enough from her thoughts and she calmed down to focus on him.

"Come on, I have an idea." With a nod of his head, he tugged on her hand. Taking a deep breath, he darted into the throngs of people. Mari was sure to stay close. His reassuring grip locked onto her palm. It felt so nice that she couldn't help but smile. The density of the people dispersed the further up the boardwalk they got. He was taking her away from the amusement park end. As long as he focused on the task at hand, he felt his anxiety lessen with each step.

The large marquee and flashing lights were like a beacon. It beckoned them to partake of the delights within.

"An arcade?" Mari glanced at Ben with a laugh.

"Why not? Our mini-golf competition was fun. This might be a little…less dangerous. Hopefully no flying balls." He teased her and she scrunched her shoulders. She bashfully remembered her rouge shot that almost took him out.

"I think you just like winning. Or well…attempting to." Mari teased right back with a bite of her lower lip. "So we should avoid the ball games. Although…I am really good at Skeeball."

"Maybe we should play something you aren't good at."

"Oh, scared of some healthy competition again, McGregor?"

"Fine. Let's go see just how good you are then." He challenged with a quirk of a smile. Once he loaded up a game card for the two of them, they headed over to the wall lined with the machines. He scanned the card for two lanes next to each other. "Hope you can put your balls where your mouth is." Ben was completely oblivious to how vulgar his threat was as Mari erupted into a fit of laughter. She bent over as she gasped and tried to catch her breath from her mirth.

"Ben, do you even listen to yourself sometimes?"

"I do. Why?" He looked upon her in confusion as she continued to laugh as tears formed in her eyes.

"*Put your balls where your mouth is?* Ben, you're lucky there aren't any kids near us."

His look remained locked in puzzlement with a cock to his head as he mouthed the words that she had stressed upon. Mari knew the moment the realization about what he said hit him. His eyes went wide and a pink blush rose to his cheeks.

"Ah…well…forgive me."

"Oh god, no. That shit was hilarious." Turning to her game, Mari got into her stance and readied her arm. "Watch me fondle my balls!" Stooping down with a laugh, she rolled the ball up the ramp and effortlessly into the 40-point ring. Ben chuckled as his blush continued with her endless double entendres. Yet another moment he wasn't going to live down.

Skeeball was more in Ben's wheelhouse and the two tied after playing ten games. They were breathless with laughter. Ben had attempted to cheat the system a few times while Mari's tried-and-true method of rolling the ball continued to work out well. Playing the game together made the world melt away for a bit.

Ripping off their dispersed tickets, Mari was claimed the winner. As she had three more tickets than Ben. The pair made their way around the arcade as they tried out most of the two-player games or watched each other play. There was so much laughter. It made Mari forget all about being stuck in her book. She was genuinely having fun.

The ease between them was almost second nature at this point. Ben found himself reaching down to clasp her hand as they walked from game to game. Mari didn't protest as she enjoyed the attention and the calming effect that it had on her. It seemed to her that Ben was benefiting from their arrangement as much as she was. With each date, he had come further out of his shell. By the end of the evening, Mari could see the appeal of Ben's true self. Any woman would be lucky to date him.

The arcade was quieting down as the evening grew late. Ben encouraged Mari to go ahead and cash in their tickets and pick whatever she wanted. Casting him a curious brow she shrugged and wandered over to the prize desk to peruse the glass case. Ben had been eying up the claw machines all evening. He was decent at them, but it had been some time since he had played one.

There was a particular one that caught his attention. It was one of the more expensive claw machines. But inside was a rather adorable plush white unicorn stuffed animal. He wanted nothing more than to win one and surprise Mari with it. Shoving a $5 bill into the machine, he readied himself at the controls.

He was on his third attempt when Mari wandered back over with a handful of candy.

"I hope you don't mind I got us a snack. I gave the rest of the tickets to the kids behind me. They need sugar more than we do." She laughed before she got distracted by what Ben was doing. "Oh my gosh, Ben. No one wins those."

Keeping his gaze on the machine, Ben smirked with a casual shrug. "It's always worth a try." Ripping open one of the packages of Starburst, she popped one into her mouth. She chewed as she watched the plush toy fall back to the depths of the machine. Ben grumbled but he still had two more tries. He was so close, more determined now than ever.

Chuckling, Mari wandered off to deposit her trash in the nearest receptacle. As she turned around to head back to Ben, she was met square in the face with the soft white belly of a stuffed unicorn. With a startle, she choked a bit on the remnants of the candy in her mouth.

"I won this for you." The voice seemed to come from the animal, but Mari knew that honeyed accented voice anywhere. She took a step back and gazed at the sweet critter with its luminescent fur and horn to match. Shoving the rest of the candy into her purse, she tenderly reached up to clutch the prize in her hands. She pulled it to her and promptly smothered the gift in a fierce hug as she buried her face in the fur.

Ben beamed as Mari clutched at the sweet token. But the sudden sniffle from her made his heart seize and he worried that he had upset her.

"Oh, Ben…" She murmured with an emotional warble to her voice as the tears started to fall. It was stupid to get so emotional over a damn stuffed animal. Yet there she was, sobbing over the gift. "I love it. Holy shit I love it so much." There was a muffled choked sob as she started to laugh. "I'm sorry, it's stupid to get all weepy over an arcade prize."

"Not at all. I'm glad you like it." The smile he offered was sweet and reassuring. He took such delight in her joy. As much as he didn't want the evening to end it was getting late and Ben had to be up for work the next morning. "Should we head home?" Mari nodded as she sniffled. He smoothed his hand across the small of her back to gently guide her out of the arcade.

Chapter Sixteen

The boardwalk was quieter as some shops had begun closing up for the night. There was an occasional burst of laughter from a group of teens that whizzed by on bikes. But for the most part, it was much calmer. The pair walked in silence and Ben found himself unable to stop grinning.

Mari calmed down from her surprise with his reassuring touch and the pair moved back to holding hands. She continued to clutch the stuffed animal close to her chest. From time to time, she would bury her face in it to hide her smile. The date had been so simple, but it had been utterly perfect. For the last few hours, she had actually forgotten that this was all a fake premise in order for her to write a book. It actually felt…real. Or well, whatever she thought a real relationship would feel like. It wasn't until his car was on the highway that Ben broke the silence.

"I had a lot of fun tonight."

"I did too. Thank you." Mari smiled to herself. "Best date I've ever been on. Real or fake. Although I keep saying that don't I?"

Ben's shoulders sagged a bit at the mention of the fake date. On the bright side, she did admit to having the best date of her life. And it just so happened to be with him.

"Maybe we should make the arcade a regular thing?"

"It was fun, but we should keep trying new things in this experiment." Mari reminded him and his shoulders sank.

"O-Oh, right. Good point."

The quiet came back over the car and she fidgeted with the unicorn in her lap. Ben had gone out of his way that evening to make Mari feel good. He had used all the things he had compiled from their earlier conversations all on one date. Now she wanted to attempt to ask him out for another one. She felt it was only fair as he had been the one to extend the invitation before.

"What are you doing for the Fourth?"

"Of July?"

"Yes, that Fourth." She chuckled. "America's Independence Day."

"Oh, right. Um…well, the library will be closed. So…I'll probably be home reading."

"Well…do you want to be my date to Shannon's barbeque?" Mari cautiously glanced at him from the corner of her eye. Her question had taken him by surprise. Him? Around her friends? "You don't have to if you don't-"

"Yes." Ben looked over to her with a half-smile and a nod. "Yes, I will go." She mirrored his subtle nod in acknowledgment. Her attention turned back to the stuffed animal in her lap as she smiled to herself. Shannon had asked her, well, teased her, about bringing Ben to her annual get-together. Despite Mari denying her interest in him, Shannon had insisted that, either way, he could come as her date.

"Goodnight, Ben. Thanks for a fun night." Mari turned to him with a warm and genuine smile as he pulled up along the street by the back stairs behind the bakery.

"Let me at least walk you to your door." He offered with a hopeful glint in his eyes.

"Oh…sure." With a dry swallow, she nodded as he got out of the car and wandered over to her side. With a quick shove into her purse, she grabbed a handful of the candy they had won. She dispensed it behind her back for him to find later. After all, half the bounty was his. Ben kindly opened the car door for her. She flashed him a thankful smile as she slipped out the door and over to the stairs, still clutching her coveted prize.

Following a step behind her, the pair climbed the stairs to the small balcony. Mari reached out and put her key in the lock but paused. The evening had been one to remember. She didn't want to jinx it by not ending it the exact same way as their last date had ended. The only sure way she could cure her writer's block again was to kiss him.

In a breathless spin, she turned to him. Clutching his shirt in her hands, she pulled him against her. In one breath she captured his lips. This kiss was completely different from the agreed-upon one from their last date. Mari wanted to know what it felt like to catch him off guard. She wanted to kiss him hard and deep. To kiss him in such a way that she could accurately capture a similar moment with her characters. This was the spice factor that everyone wanted. And what a spice it was.

Mari felt the heat lick long and slow from her lips and throughout her extremities. It made her heart race and stall all at once in an unbridled contradiction. Her brain cried out for him to touch her, caress her. To somehow return the heat that she felt radiating from his mouth.

"S-Sorry…" She breathed out against his mouth as she pulled away in a perplexed daze. "I-I-I just…wanted to feel what a…passionate kiss was like…" The words trailed off as her eyes shyly flickered to his.

The kiss had left Ben stunned. She had taken him by complete surprise. Any hesitation or shyness was gone. Instead, there was just a man standing in front of a woman that wanted him.

With a firm step forward, his lean body pressed her back against her front door. A small squeak escaped her mouth. The swiftness of his hands cupping her jaw quieted her for only a moment before his mouth descended.

It was so quick and uninhibited. The slow and meandering fire that Mari had started, blew straight into a wild inferno. His body was so hard and warm against hers as she submitted herself to his attentions. His lips slanted and moved with subtle grace against her mouth. Caressing and coaxing out some sort of suppressed yearning. Now this was the passionate kiss that she had been after.

"Did that suffice…?" Ben murmured against her lips. He slowly pulled away, pressing his forehead to hers. Mari could hardly remember her full name, let alone muster up the words to answer him. The two stood in silence, still tangled in each other's arms as they caught their breath. There was something so intoxicating about this moment. Something not even the gifted writer could find an easy way to explain.

"G-Goodnight, Ben…" She whispered hoarsely. Blinking, Ben took that as his cue to leave. He lingered there, on her threshold, like there was some small sliver of him that wished she would have invited him inside. With one final caress against her cheek, he pulled away. He descended the stairs but was sure to cast her one last glance before heading to his car.

Chapter Seventeen

Mari had been too in awe after her last date with Ben to spend the night writing All she wanted to do was lounge in bed and relive every second of the evening over and over again. She wished to commit the date to the deepest crevices of her memory. He had been the perfect gentleman. So warm and inviting, and not to mention loads of fun. She had laughed countless times and smiled until her cheeks hurt. When he handed her the stuffed animal, she had come completely unglued.

Perhaps it wasn't fair. She was training Ben to do everything *she* liked. She needed to be teaching him about all potential dates and what to do. To take notes of their wishes and desires. All the while he continued to be his usual awkwardly sweet self.

The date worked like a charm, and she felt inspired once again. More so than the last date. Today was the last full day off for the week before Shannon needed her back in the bakery. Even with the extra seasonal help during peak season, it was busy for the first three hours of the day. Mari always offered to stay with Shannon and let the younger employees head out to enjoy the beach. It was the least she could do for her friend while she got a free beach condo out of it.

With an open day, it made the most sense to go to the library and at least attempt to type something. She had to do it while the excitement and emotion were still fresh in her mind from their date. As much as she wanted to lie in bed, hugging a pillow in her dreamy state, she needed to work.

Ben waited anxiously for her that morning. Like Mari, he had spent the better part of the night reflecting on their time together. Especially the duo of embraces they shared on her front porch. The thought of them still brought the heat to his chest. Those kisses with Mari were unlike anything he had ever experienced with anyone. Is that what love was supposed to feel like?

Love?

He had only met her a month and a half ago in mid-May and it was now barely July. To speak of such nonsense was falling back to his terrible needy habits of the past. The ones that scared off his last few partners. Those of which had been brave enough to stick around, despite his awkward nature. Maybe it was just desire. He had never felt it this strongly with any real person. A few fictional heroines had brought him close, but the notion faded as quickly as soon as he finished the book.

He knew he was breaking his own rule, but he had stopped for coffee that morning. The restless night had done him in. He hesitated for a split second but purchased an extra one for Mari. She was fond of her lattes. Every morning he watched her suck down the contents of her cup before she entered the library.

If their last date had been as successful as he had thought, she would be there hopefully at any minute. The date before last night's had put her creative mind in overdrive. She had arrived at the library, bouncing and excited from the swirl of words and ideas in her head. Today she was running a few minutes behind her usual window. He slipped into the tiny break room, which was more of a glorified supply closet, to heat up her coffee. Just in case.

With the beeping of the microwave, he missed the front door chime. As he wandered back out into the main library, he spotted her settling into her usual spot. Fearing that her coffee had become lukewarm, he hurried to catch her before she put her headphones back on. Careful not to spill her hot coffee, he kept his torso rigid as his legs took long quick strides over to her.

"Mari! Good morning. I got this for you." He had a whole adorable little speech planned. But the moment he was in her orbit, it all went out the window in an inelegant tumble of words. His sudden appearance startled her. She jumped in surprise, almost knocking the cup out of his hands.

"Oh! Ben! Morning." Mari clutched her hand against her chest as she tried to calm her racing heart. Despite almost scaring her half to death, he still held out his offering of the coffee cup. "Y-You got me coffee?" She could feel her chest tightening up from the unexpected gesture. With a quick laugh, she tried to dispel it as she teased him. "Isn't that breaking a rule?"

"I think you're worth breaking a few rules for." The words were meant to be completely innocent, but they caused Mari's cheeks to flush. How did this woman cause him to speak without thinking? His issue had always been that he over-thought everything. Every response, every gesture, every movement. Most of the time to the point where he ended up saying nothing.

"Oh…well…thank you then." A breathless smile flashed across her face as she reached out to grab the cup. In a split second of thought, she leaned in the rest of the way and brushed a kiss against the bearded scruff of his cheek. Now it was Ben's turn to blush. "I think we are pulling off the couple thing quite well, don't you?" She added softly.

"Y-Yes…I think so." Ben nodded as he watched Mari carefully settle into her chair and open up her laptop.

"Maybe the real test would be if we can fool Shannon's friends and family into believing we really are a couple." The words came out as a casual observation while she eyed her document. But what she said made the breath stall uncomfortably in Ben's chest.

"O-Oh…uh…s-sure. Right."

"You are still planning on coming, right?" She cast him a side glance as she hunched over her laptop. "I wasn't kidding. The invitation was genuine."

"I wouldn't miss it." Ben gave her a smile that she returned with delight before she slid her headphones on. As he turned away, his hands slipped into his pockets. Inside the one pocket, he thoughtfully fidgeted with one of the pieces of candy she had left for him in his car.

Chapter Eighteen

Mari had invited Ben to park at the bakery and walk down to Shannon's house with her to attend the picnic. He arrived wearing a polo shirt tucked into khaki shorts and boat shoes. While it was a bit pretentious, he looked handsome in his nerdy glory. Mari had opted for another breezy sundress. It was long and ruffled in a shade of blue that almost matched the cloudless sky. While Ben enjoyed looking at her wearing such a frock, he had to be mindful of where his thoughts wandered off to. Especially since they were heading into public with people they knew.

"You look nice, Ben." Mari offered as they stepped down onto the sidewalk from the back stairs to her apartment. Without missing a beat, she hooked her arm around the crook of his. Ben dipped his chin as he smiled to himself.

"Are my outfit choices improving?"

"Little by little." Mari teased with a laugh.

"Maybe one of our dates should be you taking me clothing shopping." He offered as he chuckled.

"Hey…that's not a bad idea. I don't think I ever went shopping with a man before. Could prove interesting. Or hilarious. Or both."

"You wouldn't make me try on anything ghastly, would you?"

"Only for comedic purposes." She admitted before dissolving into giggles.

The pair stepped up to the back gate of Shannon's home. With the success of the bakery, her parents bought and fixed up one of the duplexes on the island. It was only a few blocks down from the storefront. They lived on one side and Shannon and Luke on the other. It had taken almost a decade for them to finish both projects, but the homes had turned out quite lovely. They were one of the few year-round residents. Instead of the usual pebbled landscape, they opted to have actual grass in their yard. Which made a fine landscape for a lively 4th of July party.

Mari had always adored Shannon's mom and dad. They had become something like a second set of parents since hers passed. Mrs. Kohler was a petite and slightly rotund woman with a flurry of short white hair. Her husband was taller but completely bald with the kindest face. As she opened the gate, they were the first to greet her and Ben.

"Mari! You've been here over a month already and haven't even stopped by."

"I'm sorry Mrs. Kohler. Writing books takes a lot out of me." Mari shrugged as the missus pulled her in for a hug.

"Writing another bestseller, eh?" Mr. Kohler offered a warm smile and less scorn than his wife with his approving nod.

"Always trying!"

It was then that their attention drifted to a rather forlorn-looking Ben. He had moved to stand behind Mari.

To use her as a sort of human shield against the onslaught of potential greetings.

"Mr. McGregor, nice of you to join us." It was Mr. Kohler who first acknowledged him. He offered his hand in greeting. With a hard swallow, Ben stepped up to the man and shook his hand firmly. "You've been a staple of this community for years." The compliment brought a small smile to Ben's face, and he offered an appreciative nod.

"T-Thank you for the best scones on the island, sir."

Mr. Kohler erupted into jovial laughter and clapped him on the shoulder. "I'm glad to hear that my daughter and her husband are still making everything with our recipes!" The volume of his voice had increased for the sole reason of attracting Shannon's attention.

"Yes, Dad. Everything is still the same." Shannon sauntered over with an exaggerated eye roll. "Now can you let my guests actually breathe a minute before you interrogate them further? Luke needs your help on the grill anyway." Mr. Kohler nodded with a chuckle as he took his daughter's leave and pulled his noisy wife along with him to assist with the festivities.

"T-Thank you for inviting me." Ben was the first to speak which shocked both Shannon and Mari. He usually hesitated.

"Of course, Ben! It's nice to see you out of your natural habitat for once." She shot him a wink before turning to Mari. "Well, you know the place. The food should be done in the next hour or so. There's cornhole and lawn darts or you two can just hide in a corner."

Mari's eyes went wide, and she jabbed her friend in the ribs with her elbow. Ben couldn't help but snort nervously. No wonder Shannon and Mari were friends. They had the same snide sense of humor.

"Oh, shut it."

"Just keep the making out to a minimum." The tease was abrupt as she turned to mingle with her other guests. Which left Mari and Ben with a mutual bright flush on their cheeks. Clearing her throat, she turned to Ben. She wanted to at least lessen the tension of making a public appearance.

"Want to play cornhole?"

The pair settled into the corner of the yard with the games and quickly occupied themselves. The first game of cornhole was close but Ben had finally managed to win a game against Mari. The win helped relax him and soon they were deep in their playful taunts and quips of conversation. They were so absorbed with each other that no one wandered over to make small talk and interrupt their obvious fun.

As the sun began to set, Shannon walked around to light the tiki torches while Luke called out that the grill was ready. The party food was all lined up on folding tables with festive plastic tablecloths. The pair had to face the buffet along with the other guests and any curious questions.

"So, Mari. How long have you and Ben been dating?" Of course, the question Mari had been trying to avoid came from Mrs. Kohler, who was the town's mom. She always had to know all the town gossip and news. Mari wanted to steer clear of any potential awkwardness. All she was willing to offer were short and concise answers, and to avoid the truth as much as possible.

"A month."

"Oh, that's nice dear." Mrs. Kohler spooned some potato salad on her plate and Mari thought she was in the clear. "You make the cutest couple. Be sure to invite us to the wedding." The mere fact that she said it so nonchalantly made Mari balk and drop the tongs. She glanced over to

Ben who had turned white as a sheet. The pair thought they had been completely innocent-looking with their interactions. Perhaps even a bit distant from each other with their public display of affection. Despite all that, it seemed that something between them had caught Mrs. Kohler's attention.

"Uh…sure…" At that point, Mari and Ben were ready to find that dark corner that Shannon had teased them about earlier. Mari made a beeline for the empty knotted rope hammock in the corner by the cornhole area. She dropped herself carefully onto the hammock and held it still for Ben to ease down onto it. They sat in silence as they got their plates in order.

"I believe we have them fooled."

"Fooled enough at least. Maybe too much. I'm not exactly sure where Mrs. K got that daft notion from." As Mari bit into her hamburger, she wracked her brain with all of the moments between her and Ben at the barbecue. They had just been playing cornhole. Maybe she touched his arm a few times. She even said some funny competitive quips that he laughed at. But it was nothing that would make the average person think that they were more than just casually dating, friends even.

"I suppose it means that our arrangement is working. We are even convincing random people." Ben smiled but it was emotionless as he stared down at his plate. He made sure to hide the disappointment in his eyes. She offered a subtle nod and took another bite of her burger.

The two ate in silence, unknowingly snuggled together on the hammock in the growing darkness. While the picnic date may have been a good idea in hindsight, neither of them was having much fun anymore. There were too many thoughts swimming about in their heads. Mari distracted herself with plotting out the climax of her book and trying to ignore Mrs. Kohler's words. But it wasn't working. She needed to get out of there, lest it get any more awkward.

"Do you want to go see the fireworks?" Mari suggested as she shuffled around the remaining few chips on her plate. As much as she loved Shannon, the party wasn't cutting it for her anymore. From the looks of it, Ben wasn't exactly enjoying it to the fullest extent either.

Of all the years Mari had come to stay at the beach, she always avoided the week of the 4th. It was due to the fact of the sheer number of tourists that were there on holiday. The crowds were everywhere, and she never wanted to bother. The pre or postseason crowds were more her speed. Despite the crowds, she was always bummed to miss out on fireworks over the ocean.

"You mean we can leave?" Ben asked, hopeful as he adjusted the plate in his lap.

"Hell yes. Let's go. I'll make the excuse." The pair rose one at a time rather uneasily from the hammock. Ben dispensed of their plates as Mari wandered over to Shannon and Luke with her thanks and to say goodbye. Even in the dim lighting, Ben could see Shannon giving him a curious look over Mari's shoulder. "Okay, let's get the hell out of here," Mari whispered as she briskly walked past Ben. He fell in line right behind her.

A few guests waved and shouted their farewells. The pair returned them without a word as they slipped outside of the fence. Once they were on the other side, Mari let out a long sigh.

"Well, that was more awkward than it needed to be." Ben laughed with a nod in agreement as he glanced over at her. She was already more visibly relaxed, as was he. There was even a pep in her step as they walked in the direction of the beach. "I'm so excited for these damn fireworks." Her exclamation came out of nowhere as she had turned rather giddy. With her child-like excitement, he couldn't help but smile.

"Have you been to the fireworks at the beach before?"

"No, never! But I always wanted to. I never had a good enough reason to stay." With a quick glance over at Ben, she continued. "I always thought fireworks over the water would be magical. Have you gone to see them?"

"Nah. I never did bother."

"Oh well, it's a first for both of us then. Pop each other's cherries."

"Pop...*what?*" The look he gave her was quizzical as he cocked his head in question.

"Oh, come on, Ben. You know..." There was subtle bugging of her eyes as she gestured wildly into the air. "Popping your cherry?" The unchanged stare that he offered made Mari hesitate. "What, you've never heard that expression before?"

"Should I have?"

"I mean...maybe... I don't know what they call 'losing your virginity' in wherever you're from."

Ben stumbled a bit on the sidewalk. "I'm sorry?" Mari burst out laughing at his naivety.

"It's called 'popping one's cherry' when you lose your virginity. Or also...when you try something new for the first time."

"That is...odd."

"I know, but it's funnier the more you think about it."

The pair meandered down the sandy ramp between the dunes to walk onto the beach. The holiday festivities and best viewing area were down by Surfside Park. That also meant more people. Down on this end of the beach, there were only a few people sprinkled sporadically throughout. For the most part, they had the beach to themselves.

Mari spotted one of the lifeguard chairs. Like the others, it had been dragged back to sit by the dunes until the next lifeguard posting. Since she had neglected to bring a blanket, and neither of them was fond of sand, she thought it was as good a place as any to sit and view the fireworks. Ben was about to open in mouth in protest but thought better of it. No one would need the chairs at that time of night, so he climbed up after her.

It was a bit chillier being a few feet up in the air. Mari scooted in next to Ben's warmth as soon as he settled down. He hesitated before timidly wrapping his arm around her bare shoulders. Mari felt the heat rise to her cheeks as he rounded the palm of his hand around her arm. The warmth of his touch flooded her, warding off the chilly air.

"I was thinking."

"Oh?" Ben turned to her as his brows softened, his attention piqued.

"About our next date."

"Oh."

"Maybe we should have a movie night. Or game night. At one of our places."

"Like a pajama party of sorts?" The wheels were turning as he looked at her, in an attempt to understand her idea. "Couples do that sort of thing. Don't they?"

"I mean yeah…sure. But I don't think pajamas are usually involved, Ben." Mari grinned as she bit her lip, shooting him a quick but teasing glance.

"Oh. *Oh.*" He chuckled nervously as a blush bloomed across his face. "Right. Obviously."

"Well…uh…not that we have to do that or anything." She quickly added. "We can make it a chill evening. Watch a movie, and have pizza delivered. I think we might need a break from the public eye for a while." There was a soft chuckle as she looked down at her hands that fidgeted in her lap.

"That would be nice."

"We have to keep my writing mojo going somehow."

Ben opened his mouth to retort, but the fireworks began to explode in the night sky. They leaned against the stiff angled seat of the wooden lifeguard chair to partake of the show. The spectacle was stunning. The bright explosions of color lit up the darkness as if it were day. They reflected in a warbled blur across the gently rolling waves of low tide.

A grin was plastered across Mari's face as she leaned a bit more against Ben. The crackles and pops sounded up and down the beach. She was completely engrossed in the sparkling magic. But not Ben. He was distracted by other means. His mind was stuck on thoughts of the woman next to him. Suddenly something had caught his eye.

"Mari, look." Ben reached out to gesture up the beach to their left. His hand cut through her line of sight and broke her from her gazing stupor. From their vantage point, they could see a whole number of fireworks displays up the Northern coast. It was clear all the way to the outward curve of Atlantic City. Her eyes moved to where he pointed and a gasp of delight left her mouth.

"Oh, my god. How incredible!" She turned her gaze back to him to discuss the spectacle. The words dissipated instantly with how close Ben's mouth was to hers. She wasn't interested in the fireworks anymore. The sudden urge to kiss Ben overshadowed all else. "W-What do you think about…us…practicing kissing? Sure, beats practicing on a watermelon." Ben blinked at her as he attempted to contemplate exactly what she meant.

"A watermelon?" The question came with a laugh.

"Isn't that what teenagers use? Or a pillow. Or their hand." Mari rambled and found herself trying to make the idea more enticing. "We both have to make sure we are good kissers. Like…*really* good kissers."

"Ah…" She was making Ben fluster again. "Well…uh…I suppose."

"Then kiss me. Fireworks at night by the beach are pretty damn romantic. At least we have the scene set." Her voice was breathy and seemingly desperate.

This kiss, like all the others before it, brought that same flood of warmth and delight. So, the others weren't a fluke. Ben was already an expert-level kisser. At least by Mari's standards. He could have been that good of a kisser all along and no one ever bothered to tell him. Maybe when they had the privacy of one of their apartments, that would allow more time for teaching and critique. But for now, Mari wanted to enjoy this one in all its awkward glory.

Chapter Nineteen

Mari knocked on Ben's condo door. The butterflies were fluttering wildly in her stomach as she stood rocking back and forth on her heels. She felt her heart seize as soon as the deadbolt clicked. They had agreed upon meeting up at Ben's place. Mari suggested they meet Tuesday night since the bakery was closed on Wednesdays.

The moment Ben opened the door he erupted in amused laughter.

"Ah so…pajama party it is." His ocean-blue eyes gave her a good once-over. Starting at her plush bunny slippers up to her floral cotton shorts. All before residing a bit too long on the scoop neckline of her t-shirt. With a dry swallow, he recentered himself. Smiling, he invited her inside.

"Well…it sounded fun. Plus, it gave me a reason to put my PJs on early." Stepping inside, she plopped a box of movie butter microwave popcorn into his arms before sauntering into his apartment. As a writer, she always liked to study people's living habitats. It helped inspire some quirks for characters in her books. With Ben's odd personality, she was more than a little curious to study his place.

"I guess I am overdressed?" Ben joked as he closed the door. Mari glanced over at him with a laugh as she gave him an overly dramatic once-over.

"Seems like it, McGregor."

"Thanks for the popcorn. I'm sure this will come in handy in a bit. Shall we order pizza? I…wasn't exactly sure what kind you like so I didn't want to be presumptive and order ahead."

"Oh…well. I'm not super picky." Mari shrugged as she wandered the long way through his living room and into the kitchen. "Mushrooms, green peppers, and sausage are my favorite. But plain cheese is fine."

Ben smiled as he watched her. "That actually sounds delicious. Let's go with that." Mari's brows perked on her forehead with delighted surprise. It was rare that anyone agreed to her desired pizza toppings. "I can order if you want to make popcorn?"

With a nod, Mari ripped open the box of popcorn. She set about figuring out how to work his microwave to make the snack. Ben grabbed his cell phone to order from the local shop and wandered into his bedroom to make the call. It took her a moment, but she finally figured out the popcorn setting and sent the packet spinning. Her eyes moved to survey his condo more closely. It was simple but cozy. There was masculine leather furniture and an entire wall of floor-to-ceiling bookshelves filled to the brim with books.

With her curiosity peaked, she wandered over and scanned through the organized stacks. She chuckled to herself. Of course, the librarian would have all his books sorted in alphabetical order by author and title. Her heart raced a bit when she then noticed every single one of her books lined up in a row on his shelf.

She shot a quick glance in Ben's direction, but he was still in his room. Since the coast was clear, she plucked the first book she ever wrote off the shelf. Reaching into her purse, she pulled out her pen and wrote a quick inscription on the title page addressed to Ben. Maybe he would find it one day or perhaps someone else would. Either way, the thought of it made her smile. She returned the book back onto the shelf as the microwave beeped.

"I've got it," Ben called out as he was already grabbing a bowl from one of the cupboards. He had come out of his bedroom dressed in his pajamas and Mari smiled to herself. With the plaid flannel bottoms and plain V-neck t-shirt, he looked comfortable. Although the shirt looked a size too small. The neckline dipped low enough and it provided her an enticing peek at his auburn chest hair.

As a blush rose to her cheeks, Mari took the liberty to plop down on the one side of the sofa. It was the end that had a plush blanket draped across the cushion. She could still feel the chill of the leather through the blanket. It felt soothing against her flushed skin. Ben wandered over to her with a smile and placed the bowl of popcorn on the rustic wood coffee table.

"Would you like something to drink? I did take the liberty of acquiring your favorite hard cider."

The mention of alcohol made her cringe. But she was touched that he went out of his way to pick out something she liked.

"Yeah. I will take one. But just one!" She warned and Ben chuckled.

"Duly noted." He wandered back to the kitchen, dipped into the fridge to pull out two hard ciders, and opened both. "Pizza should be here in half an hour." Handing Mari her bottle he settled onto the couch on the complete opposite end of her.

"Ben."

"What?"

Mari overexaggerated the beckoning gesture with her head and eyes as she glanced between herself and Ben.

"Don't you think we should actually sit next to each other?"

"Oh. Uh. Right." Ben moved to the middle couch cushion, and she laughed.

"You do understand the concept of snuggling? Right?" She teased and a pink tinge rose to his cheeks. "We should at least attempt to try it out. I believe that is the point of movie nights."

"I thought it was the lack of pajamas?" Ben asked innocently and Mari burst out laughing. "Oh. Wait." The red blush spread from his cheeks straight up to the tips of his ears.

"Anyway." Mari rolled her eyes with a grin. "What movie should we watch?"

"From what I researched…horror movies seem to be the consensus." Ben was thankful for the change in subject to avoid any further embarrassment. Although the disgusted face Mari presented suggested that he had made a move in the wrong direction. "Am I incorrect?"

"I mean it may be true for most couples, but I hate horror movies. Or anything scary for that matter."

"Ah well, I am relieved to hear you say that. As I am not fond of them either."

"Well…the backup would be a romantic movie. Do you have an aversion to those?"

"I do not."

"Good." Mari settled back against the plush leather sofa with a satisfied sigh. "Maybe we can even learn something. Or critique it."

Ben chuckled. "All right. Let's see what is available."

The two spent the next few minutes scrolling through the various streaming services that Ben had. They had gone through a dozen or so titles before finally settling on one that neither had seen before. It sounded like it had a tinge of humor to it. But the sudden ring of the doorbell halted Ben from pressing play.

"Good timing."

The pair of them dove into the pizza and popcorn. The casualness of the meal was perfect. There was a good bit of mutual commentary on the movie as they ate. They each took turns poking fun at the female main character. She was overly whiny about not being able to find a man. Sure, finding that one person you are meant to be with was no easy task, but it was not worth obsessing over. In her own dating experience, Mari was content with the mantra that if it were meant to be, it would happen.

Wiping her hands on a napkin, Mari downed the rest of her hard cider before tucking her legs up beside her. Mari cast a quick glance over to Ben. He looked rather comfortable with his arm outstretched along the back of the couch. There was an amused smirk on his lips that caused his beard to twitch.

Mari had been hemming and hawing over being the first to make a move or not. Or even broach the subject again. The whole date idea of hers had an ulterior motive. She needed to snuggle with Ben. The characters in her book were attempting something similar to their current situation. She had no idea how to start or what a couple would actually do.

Ben turned to look at Mari and caught her in the middle of her thoughtful stare. With a blush on his cheeks, he cocked a brow at her.

"Do I have something on my face?"

"I want you to snuggle with me."

"Now…?" Ben bristled.

"Why not? That's what a couple should be doing while they watch the movie, right?"

"I…suppose so?"

Mari scooted herself over in Ben's direction and he froze, unsure of what to do. An aggravated sigh escaped her lips before she pursed them in her frustration. Snuggling always seemed to be a bony tangle of limbs. How did anyone find that appealing?

"How do couples actually cuddle on the couch? I feel like it would be uncomfortable."

It was as if the romance gods were on their side. The movie flashed to a scene very much like the one they were trying to attempt. Ben studied the characters on the television for a moment before glancing at his hands. The male had placed his arm around the female as she leaned in.

"Perhaps we should just do what they're doing?" Ben offered. He adjusted the positioning of his arms to place the one closest to Mari around her shoulders. She nodded before scooting up as close as she could manage to him. Draping her folded knees over his lap, she snuggled into the crook of his arm. To her surprise, it was comfortable.

"This…this actually isn't so awful." With a nod Ben kept his studying gaze locked on the screen. He wanted to take in every movement that the love interest made toward the woman. The characters remained locked in their embrace for a while as they talked. That was until the man took the opportunity to lean in and begin his advance to seduce her.

Without moving his head, Ben glanced at Mari. She still had her eyes on the movie, trying to commit the playout of the scene to memory. If she and Ben couldn't figure it out, at least there was something she could visually fall back on. The advice of following the movie characters' lead was circling around in his head. There was no better way to learn than by imitating real life. Er well, in this case, a movie.

Leaning in, his eyes darted between her cheek and neck to formulate an attack plan of sorts. Mari felt his fingertips shakily graze along the edge of her jaw. The touch distracted her long enough so he could press a tender kiss against her neck. Her inhale was sharp as the contact was surprisingly intimate. With her reaction, Ben hesitated but did not move from where he was.

"A-Am I doing it wrong…?" His worried whisper was hot against her skin. She attempted to swallow down the wild flush of heat. A thousand alarms were screaming inside her head. Some were urging her to pull away, but the others were wanting more.

"N-No…" The warbling whisper was confirmation enough for Ben. He eased back into lavishing soft and slow kisses against her throat. Skin that he had yet to taste until that moment. Her perfume was stronger against her pulse point. He breathed it in deeply. She was so warm and sweet. He couldn't help himself from partaking with an open mouth.

Mari's hand shot out to grip Ben's thigh as she felt overcome by a whole jumble of sensations across her body. She felt his sharp inhalation against her skin as he hesitated. Right now, she didn't have a coherent thought in her brain. All she wanted was more.

Her hands abruptly latched onto his face, bringing his mouth to her lips. Ben made a squandered noise of surprise with her suddenness. But was easily coaxed into the embrace. Her hands slid over his shoulders to tangle her arms around his neck. She pulled him close with an aggressive desperation that seemed to have come out of nowhere.

The moment his hands smoothed around her lower back to pull her in tighter against him, all hell broke loose. With a further twist of her body, she maneuvered her legs underneath her. From there she used the leverage to press Ben down against the couch. She ignored his strangled noise as she laid her body out atop him. Without letting him catch his breath she slanted her mouth firmly against his.

It didn't take much for Ben to fall under her spell. His hands moved across the breadth of her back as his lips caressed hers in reply. Everything at that moment felt like heaven. Mari couldn't comprehend anything beyond the feel of his body beneath hers. The heat of his touch spread sparks throughout. Her basic sexual instinct was kicking in. It overwhelmed her all at once and she had no defenses in place to let her common sense take over. Not when everything was infiltrating her every sense with the most incredible stimulation.

Ben's consciousness had yet to completely vacate the premises. Her thighs straddled his hips, and it jolted him to sobered awareness. There were the beginnings of a straining excitement between his legs. The last thing he wanted to do was to embarrass Mari or himself with his erection. As much as he enjoyed her taking charge, he wasn't sure if he was ready for this to go further quite yet.

Sliding his hands up her sides to cup the lower part of her ribcage, he pushed her away. He regretted the motion the moment their lips separated. But he did not want to take advantage of Mari if she let herself become too vulnerable.

"M-Mari...I-" As soon as their connection severed the enchanting spell of the moment was shattered. Mari came back to consciousness as she furiously blinked away the sultry haze. She glanced down at Ben in a daze. He looked up at her with some odd mix of concern and something else that she couldn't quite put her finger on. The vision of him caged beneath her caused her to startle. She pushed herself off of him and jammed herself into the corner of the couch in embarrassment.

"Oh shit. Oh my god. Fuck. Shit. I-I'm so sorry, Ben." Her rambling was breathless and almost incoherent. Mari buried her face in her hands as her heart raced as much as her mind. "I-I don't know what came over me."

Ben sat up and tugged his shirt down over his lap as he leaned forward to press his elbows onto the top of his thighs. Clasping his hands together nervously, he stared at the floor.

"I-uh...it's alright...We are...still learning after all." He moved the tongue around his mouth in a desperate attempt to moisten the hoarseness from his voice.

"True." Mari nodded as she hugged her legs up to her chest. "But still. That-that was...a lot. I'm sorry. I can go." Reaching out to the side table, she grabbed her purse and rose from the couch to head to the front door. Ben was quick to follow. He grabbed her arm, stalling her efforts.

"I-Its fine. I mean...well...not really. I mean-" He clamped his eyes shut as he tried to get a grip on what he wanted to convey to her. "Kissing...is fine. It's...if...if we want to go further...we should...talk it out." Cautiously he opened his eyes. He was terrified that he was going to scare her off with his broken verbiage alone.

"Oh…" Her eyes were wide as she blinked at him. The inner workings of her brain were trying to reconvene behind her blank gaze. "You're talking about…sex, right?"

His Adam's apple bobbed as he thickly swallowed down his fluster. He offered a subtle nod.

"That…is an essential aspect of a relationship. Is it not?"

"Well…technically, yes…"

"So…we should communicate about it. Correct?" He was avoiding the entire point of the conversation.

"Do you want to have sex with me, Ben? Yes, or no?" Mari dramatically crossed her arms in front of her. She was over Ben dancing around the question. Most men wouldn't even bother to ask. They would take her without hesitation. Or well…at least attempt to influence the female in question in that direction. Like the sexy love interests in the romance books she sometimes read. Although if Ben took charge, as he did after their second kiss, she wasn't sure she would be able to resist again.

"I-uh…"

"Sex. Yes or no." Her patience was wearing thin as Ben began to sweat bullets.

"Uh…yes." The response was quick. His reaction after made it seem as if he regretted giving her an outright answer. "But uh… it's for your…book, right?"

"Oh." As much as she didn't want disappointment to bleed into her tone of voice, the tiniest bit did. Her book was the only reason she was in this predicament in the first place. However delicious it was becoming. Feelings could not and should not get in the middle of this. "My book. Right. Exactly."

"Your place or mine?" It was all a business deal now.

"Mine. I'll cook dinner."

"Next week?"

"Sure."
"Same time?"
"Sounds good."

And just like that, the awkward, business-like, transaction for sexual scientific research was complete. Unlike the last few dates, Mari gave him a curt nod instead of her usual goodbye kiss and escaped out his front door. Without so much as a second glance back at him.

Chapter Twenty

Mari spent the following week obsessing over her and Ben's entire conversation from their last date. Yes, that conversation. The one about sex.

Having never written anything more than some heated glances or a sultry thought, Mari was at a standstill in her debate about writing a smut scene. Especially since the last time she had actual sex was well over three years ago. A smart author would gradually add more spice to each new book they released until they were confident enough in their skill. But no, Mari had to go into a head-over-heels straight dive into exactly what her fans were craving.

It's not like she was uncomfortable writing such a thing. The anatomically correct words didn't make her erupt into giggles or blush like a Catholic nun. She thought that was a good sign at least. She had even spent an entire day researching appropriate male and female anatomy descriptors. Ones that weren't so vulgar. Heaven help her if anyone got ahold of her search history, especially after this project. They'd think she was a prude of a teenager trying to figure out sex for the first time.

The awkward encounters in her late teens and early 20s had left her anything but satisfied. But that's when no one has a grasp on decent sexual technique. Because of those disappointing partners, she moved on to settle into taking care of things herself. Which she was completely content with.

Until Ben kissed her.

How an actual person could make her loins ache was beyond her. Some of the steamy scenes in books and movies had urged her to take a little personal time here and there, but never before had a real person caused her to do so. There was this spark with Ben, this longing for more. She was certain that sex would either cure it…or make it worse.

Today was the day she would find out.

Ben was coming over to have sex.

Purely for research purposes of course.

That was if Mari could get past her brain to stop fretting about every little detail. She had barely slept the night before. Then she spent the entire day furiously cleaning every square inch of the apartment. She and Ben were only going to have sex, in one room only, to provide honest feedback to each other. It was as simple as that.

So why was she freaking out?

Half the day she wondered if she should go get a wax. Do normal people even do that? Do they wax off all the hair or leave a little? The fretting about such nonsense made no sense to her. It's not like she had to impress Ben. Or even seduce him. He was coming over as a willing participant.

In her wild cleaning spree, she had opted to make dinner in the slow cooker. Just in case they got a little sidetracked in their planned evening and forgot about dinner. It sounded like something from a cheesy 60s romantic comedy. Or maybe she was being overly hopeful.

Or physically desperate.

Or both.

The sharp knock at the door startled her from her 184th check on the status of the simmering meal. She shakily put the glass lid back down onto the cooker before glancing over at the table. It was still set from when she had put it together almost three hours prior. Maybe she should have entertained Ben at the apartment more often than before this point. Then at least she might not have gone so over the top with her preparations.

Smoothing her hands down the front of her slip dress, she stumbled over the throw rug on her way to the door. She managed to catch herself in the middle of a whirlwind of aggressive internal pep talk to get her shit together. As soon as possible.

Opening the door with a flourish, she offered Ben a breathless smile. He looked like a reflection of herself. Seemingly calm on the outside, but there was a nervous and unbridled look behind his gaze. Mari realized that she had been standing in the doorway for far too long, lost in thought, and hadn't invited him inside. Clearing her throat, she stepped off to the side and awkwardly gestured to him to come in.

"Uh…hi, Ben."

"H-Hey."

Ben arrived in khaki shorts and a plain maroon, brushed heather t-shirt. As Mari pushed the door closed, he kicked off his leather flip-flops by the door. The pair stood uneasily in the shallow foyer, unable to meet the others' gaze.

"I-It was nice of you to offer to make dinner, Mari."

"Oh…uh. You're welcome." With a blush, she shrugged her shoulders shyly. "But…I'm too nervous to eat."

"Oh?"

"I-I'd just rather get it over and done with."

"…O-Oh." Ben swallowed dryly before subtly bobbing his head. "Ah…o-o-okay. So…?"

"The bedroom?"

The food could always wait. From everything she researched to brush up on the subject of sexual acts, there was no way that it would take more than half an hour. Even with substantial foreplay. Heck, if the sex was going to be disappointing, then at least she had a solid meal and dessert to look forward to after.

"I think…I think that would be smart." Mari managed to get out, despite the croak in her voice. "I-It's through here." With a subtle nod of her head, she gave Ben the invitation to follow her. As he shoved his hands into his pockets, he fell into step behind her.

The bed looked flawless as Mari had freshly washed and remade it for the occasion. Her sheets hadn't even been remotely dirty. She assumed that Ben might be grossed out by the thought of sliding into a used bed. Why that was one of the things she fretted about, she had no idea. It could have been a scapegoat so that she could avoid the thought of being naked in front of a man for the first time in years.

Ben's eyes immediately moved to the bed where he spotted the stuffed animal that he had won for her. It had a place of honor on her bed. The sweet flutter in his heart stalled as he felt the color drain from his face. His thoughts shifted to the sole reason why she had brought him into her bedroom in the first place.

Mari walked up to the foot of the queen-sized bed before turning around to face him. This was as good of a time as ever to get started. She tossed her glasses onto the long dresser next to her. Her stomach twisted into knots as she nudged the straps of her dress over her shoulders. She let the garment fall into a deflating heap at her bare feet.

With the subtle movement of color, Ben's eyes moved back to Mari. He inhaled sharply as his body went rigid at the sight of her in only her bra and underwear. She had not been kidding about wanting to get this evening started, or well…over with. He stood transfixed by the vision of her in a matching black lace set of undergarments. It was nothing vulgar, but tasteful. Enticing.

Mari could feel the inquiring heat of his gaze while she shifted her weight back and forth from foot to foot. It was as if the movement of her body had put him in a trance. Fussing with her hair and tucking it behind her ear, she waited for him to say something. Except he didn't. He only stood there, frozen.

"I-It's your turn, Ben." At least that got him to blink. There was a bob of his Adam's apple as he timidly shuffled his way closer to her. He pulled off his glasses and gingerly discarded them next to Mari's. As soon as he came within arm's reach of her, she grabbed a hold of his shirt and tugged it up and over his head. His entire body went stiff, along with the part that was actually supposed to. This was going to be more difficult than she thought. "Relax… it's only me. Remember?"

But that was the problem. It was *her*. The woman that he had been growing increasingly more attracted to was standing before him, almost naked, in her bedroom. All while beckoning him to get undressed in her anxious impatience.

Swallowing, Ben uneasily nodded as his hands trembled with the fastener of his shorts. Her eyes were so intense, flickering up and down his body as if she was devouring him from sight alone. His breath stalled as his shorts fell slack around his hips before he nudged them to puddle at his feet. There was a quirk of a smile on her lips as she pressed herself closer to him.

Even without their bodies touching, the heat radiating off of her naked skin was intoxicating. Despite Ben being apprehensive, he couldn't help but be drawn in by her aura. His hands were shaking as they reached out to graze against the skin of her abdomen. The way her breath hitched made his eyes flash up to her face.

Her dreamy gaze led him to believe that the touch was acceptable. He caressed the quivering skin, more confident of himself with every passing moment. It drew an enticing rumble from her throat. From the visual stimuli alone, he felt himself getting harder by the second. He cursed for wearing his usual boxer briefs instead of one of his pairs of traditional boxers. At least those left him with a little more room to grow without becoming so obvious of his eager desire.

Her little noises of want were not helping the situation. With each subtle advance he had to stall his study of her body in order to get control of himself. Ben had not been with a woman in almost five years. He was a bit terrified of being out of practice. He needed to keep his excitement to a dull roar instead of an all-at-once eruption.

Mari shifted her weight every so often. It was some sort of unconscious effort to draw him in further with a jut of her chest or a subtle roll of her hips. He kept pausing at all the worst moments. It only left her body screaming for more. Despite his stopping and starting, he continued to send jolts of electricity straight between her thighs. Was she so desperate for intimacy that she was succumbing to the jerky movements of an ill-experienced man?

Maybe Ben needed a bit more encouragement. Her hands were trembling as she smoothed her palms across his chest. There was a subtle tease of chest hair against her skin, and she bit down on her flushed bottom lip. Visually, sex was great but add in the tactile and audio sensations and she fell into the best kind of sensory overload.

With a grit to her teeth, she slid her hands up to cup around the bearded edge of his jaw and pulled his face to hers. The move took him by surprise as their lips melded together. He succumbed within seconds. Little by little he relaxed into her touch. She sighed with relief into his mouth. Mari gently shifted their positions, so her legs butted up against the foot of the bed as Ben towered over her.

He was still unsuspecting, so she made her final move. Hooking her arms around his neck, she fell back onto the bed. His one hand quickly moved to support the small of her back as they descended. The other reached out to brace his fall against the bed. There was an awkward flailing of limbs, but she kept her arms locked around him. Her mouth continued to press firmly against his, so he had no means to escape.

Not that he wanted to. It was his cursed flight or fight response kicking in that caused him to writhe against her. He scrambled to straddle himself above her thighs when his pelvis fell against hers. The both of them made an awkward noise. She let him have his way in the hope that he would calm down enough to ease himself into touching her more. At least he hadn't stopped kissing her.

Ben was using his arms to keep himself propped up and above her inviting body. There was that deep and desperate ache to reach out and touch her. But every time he thought about it his brain and body seemed to flatline too close to oblivion. He was in no rush to reach his peak, especially before anything even remotely intimate started.

Keeping his lips locked with hers, he eased himself down onto the bed onto his side. His hands nudged her body to follow his orientation, which she did so eagerly. This way he could keep her at forearm's length while he tested the waters of his excitement in touching her body. With the change in position, he finally felt more at ease. Enough so that he worked his way up to his normal kissing talents.

"Ben…" Mari whispered against his mouth, almost pleading with him. She wanted him to stop being so shy and just consume her. To consume her with such a wild and fiery passion like every love interest in every romance book ever. To break out of his anxious shell and devour her completely.

It took every shred of the bravery he had left to timidly graze his fingers across the quivering skin of her abdomen. There was an approving murmur from Mari as he lingered there. He hesitated, still unsure if this was still a good idea. Her eyes had long since closed and he felt safe to turn his gaze to hers. He wanted to watch her reactions to his ministrations.

Her chest rose and fell with a hastened beat as he trailed his hand out and over to her side. Cautiously his fingers followed the curve of her side before he hesitated at the swell of her breast. Her skin was still enclosed in the lace of her bra. He wanted nothing more than to touch every inch of her naked skin. But she was moving at a speed that was too quick for him. The straining between his legs was getting out of hand. He needed to take a moment to compose himself enough lest he lose complete control of his body.

He managed to distract his thoughts with the vision of the piles of paperwork on his desk at the library. All the tasks that needed to be done in the next few days. His aching hardness relaxed some. He finally felt confident enough to slide his palm over the heft of her breast and cup it in his hand. What he didn't expect to affect him was the approving soft moan from her mouth.

There was a desperate attempt to brush away the sultry jumble of thoughts that threatened a preemptive release yet again. He tried to coax the boring work checklist back into the center of attention. All while his hand continued to caress and massage her breast. Mari was getting suspicious as he lingered longer there than necessary.

"Ben...touch me." She encouraged and opened her eyes to small slits to see what was going on with the poor man. He seemed to be hyper-focused on the work of his hand as there was a blank stare in his blue eyes. Maybe he needed a gentle redirection.

"Ben." The utterance of his name was firmer and this time it brought his eyes back up to hers. Her hands clasped his, stilling his hand against her breast. "Ben. Touch me." The quiet drew on as Mari gathered the courage to voice what she wanted. "Here."

With her raspy plea, she took and slid his hand inside the front of her panties. She had moved swiftly to avoid any protests. Shadowing her fingers over his, she urged them to slip between her folds. The sheer look of shock that blossomed over his face sent a jolt down between her legs. It continued with the graze of his middle finger against her swollen bud.

There was a throaty and warbled inhale from Ben as he awkwardly attempted to choke back a loud moan. His face twisted as if he was in pain. The tumble of noises that followed only added to that theory. The color of his skin was wildly flushed and there was a faint glisten of sweat along his brow.

Mari bit her lower lip as his fingers twitched against her. Her pleasure turned to concern as his breathing became a quick panting. If he continued on like that, he would likely hyperventilate. His eyes clamped shut as his lashes fluttered with his obvious exasperation.

"Oh god…Ben… Are you okay? I didn't hurt you, did I?" She reached up to touch his cheek and felt the trembling quiver of his clammy skin. While she knew her vaginal muscles were strong, she didn't think they were *that* strong.

Ben jumped with her questioning caress and his eyes shot open in a panic.

Oh no.

He did not just do that.

He did not orgasm from the sheer act of touching a woman's vagina.

Except that he did.

He ripped his hand away from her and sat up as he slid away. Of course, he had to go and completely mess this moment up. One that most men on the planet could have maneuvered their way through to an appropriate release. Not lose their mind, or their ejaculate, like some ill-experienced schoolboy. There was a furious and ungainly scramble off the bed as he stumbled to collect his strewn clothing.

"I-I'm, sorry, Mari. I-I…I can't do this…" He breathlessly mumbled as he tugged on his shirt and grabbed his glasses. The sticky wet mess in his boxers was uncomfortable. It fueled the terribleness of his anxiety. He needed to get out of there. And fast.

"What? Wait… Ben…hang on…!"

Slipping out of the bedroom, he made an odd, bow-legged beeline for the front door to collect his shoes. Mari grabbed her throw blanket off the foot of the bed and threw it across her shoulders. She followed after him, hoping to beat him before he made a hasty exit.

"I-I'm sorry, Mari."

Was all he could manage to say as he slammed the door behind him.

Chapter Twenty-One

Well, had been unexpected.

Hot. But unexpected.

Mari spent the better part of that night wondering what the hell she did to upset him. Where she had gone wrong. He had run off like a wounded animal and she was unsure of how to even approach him to talk about what had happened.

So, she did the most logical thing for an educated person such as herself.

She did an internet search.

Dr. Website Browser had brought up a whole bunch of ideas, embarrassing stories, and whatnot that could explain Ben's behavior. Throughout her research, the consensus seemed to all point to one thing.

He had prematurely ejaculated.

It made sense. The noises that escaped him, as his entire body shuddered and froze, were very much like… Well, it was like what she remembered of a male having an orgasm. She had been so afraid that she had hurt him. Physically or emotionally. At least this provided some sort of morbid relief.

Or did it? All she had done was put his hand down her panties. His fingers had barely grazed her vagina and he succumbed to his release. Was he so overcome with the barest touch of her that he could do nothing but orgasm? Despite feeling like utter shit that night, she now felt something of a powerful sex goddess. Once she realized what his issue had been.

Although now she had to figure out a sensitive way to approach Ben to talk about what happened. He was probably still mortified and maybe wouldn't even want to attempt to have sex with her. Hopefully, that wasn't the case. She was going to do everything in her power to convince him otherwise. Convince him, not force him. If this was something he didn't want to do with her anymore, then she would respect that. However painful it might be.

Even with the abrupt end to things, the evening in bed had been teasingly hot. Sure, Ben had been going a bit too slow for her tastes, but now she realized that she had been pressuring him to go too fast in her desperation. He needed a more timid approach. She was going to have to let him lead the timeline of events. That was if there was a next time. Either that or she would have to attempt oral sex on him to get it out of his system first. Then spend the rest of the time working him back up to his euphoria.

Sitting in her apartment was not going to do any good. Mari needed to go talk to him. She wasn't sure if he would even be willing to talk to her yet. Or ever again for that matter.

There was a sudden rapt knock at her front door. With the unexpected sound she almost dropped her coffee cup that she was about to set back down on the kitchen table. Another hasty knock made her jump again. Mari half expected it to be Shannon at the door but the last person she expected to see was the one standing on her stoop.

"Ben...?"

"Um…h-hi, Mari." The poor man couldn't even bare to look her in the eye as he fidgeted on the welcome mat. It was the middle of the day. He should be at the library. "C-Can I come in…?" With a nod, she opened the door a bit more to let him slip inside. Despite the cool breeze from the ocean side of the island, Ben was overly sweaty.

Mari had given Ben his space and avoided coming into the library for a few days. Every time he thought about his embarrassing problem, he felt sick to his stomach. That was not at all the impression he wanted to give her. He wasn't some sensitive and quivering inexperienced man. Or at the very least he didn't want to come across that way. He didn't want to disappoint Mari again. That is if she even bothered to give him a second chance.

It had taken some clear soul-searching after his incident, but he knew one thing for sure. That he would rather spend his time embarrassed, as long as it was with Mari. If their summer tryst had taught him anything, it was that he had never found someone so complex and yet enticing at the same time. Now if only he could find the courage to admit his true feelings.

They hadn't seen each other in almost a week. Ben realized that he craved being with Mari more than worrying about his embarrassment. He had to go and talk to her. That was how he ended up on her porch, a sweaty and mussed hot mess.

"Is…everything okay…?" Mari crossed her arms and kept her distance from him. He looked worse for wear as he fidgeted. "Aren't you supposed to be at the library?"

"I closed it."

"You…closed the entire library?"

"Yes."

Mari blinked as she looked at him. His answers were curt and short. Based on his tone she would have thought that she was annoying him with her questions. Even though he had been the one to show up at her door.

Instead of Ben saying what he actually wanted to tell her, he word vomited something completely different. Something he didn't think he wanted to admit to.

"W-We should try again." It wasn't what he wanted to say, but there was no going back now.

"Again...? You mean...?" Ben vigorously nodded his head as his fingers tangled and untangled from each other in his mess of anxiety. "What? Now?" Mari asked in wild surprise and Ben's response was to look like he was about ready to bolt back out the door.

"No!" He cut her off with something that was almost a shout before getting a hold of himself. "I-I mean...not now. Maybe...uh...tomorrow?" She eyed him cautiously but there was a flicker of excitement.

"Ben...are you sure you're okay? Listen if it's about the other night it-"

"It's my fault."

"No, no. Ben...not at all. It's mine. I shouldn't have pushed you so fast."

Ben had gone over to Mari's apartment with the sole notion of profusely apologizing. He wanted to apologize for his awkward and abrupt end to their, what should have been, a special evening. Instead, it was Mari who claimed fault. It threw off the entire apologetic speech that he had planned.

In fact, it made his anxiety and embarrassment deflate to almost nothing. He felt as if he could collapse from the sheer relief. Not only was she not bothered by his premature peak, but she was more than willing to try again. The realization left him tongue-tied and he swayed on his feet. Mari stepped forward to clutch onto his forearm to steady him.

"Do you want to sit down...? A glass of water or something...?"

"No...no. I should get back."

"To...the library? I thought you closed it."

"I did."

"Oh...well...okay. So...um...I'll see you tomorrow?" Mari asked, thoroughly confused but rather hopeful.

"Right. Yes." Ben nodded as he headed towards her door. "Would eight o'clock work?" Mari hurried after him so she could open the door. "No dinner."

"Ah...right. No dinner is fine." The words came out in a flustered jumble as she fumbled with the doorknob. As soon as she managed to get the door open, Ben was already outside and across the landing. "Ben," Mari called out as she bit her bottom lip. The mention of his name made him pause and he turned back to glance at her. The word vomit was bubbling up inside her. It was about to make its exuberant debut whether she liked it or not. "Please don't worry that...*thing* again. If worse comes to worst, I'll just give you a blow job first."

With that, she abruptly shut the door in her shock of saying such a thing out loud. Ben was left completely stunned on the top step.

Chapter Twenty-Two

Mari's stomach was in her throat as she stood outside of Ben's condo. She felt like everyone she had passed on her journey there had been staring at her. As if they knew exactly what they had planned. It unnerved her and she kept having to remind herself that she was a grown-ass adult. It was socially acceptable for adults to meet up for sex. Maybe not for her and Ben's specific reason, but that was just splitting hairs.

An odd sort of peace came with agreeing to sex beforehand. Much easier than dancing around the subject to encourage it to happen without sounding desperate. She had to remind herself that it wasn't even the first time that Ben had seen her in her underwear. Although, if all went well, he would be seeing her completely naked very shortly.

Why she was still nervous? She had been so close, so ready to submit herself to him before it all came crashing down in an instant. The last 24 hours had been a whirlwind of research suggestions into more ways to help Ben cope with his problem. That was if it continued to be a problem.

As she held her breath, she rapped her knuckles on the steel door. There was no going back now.

"Mari," Ben instantly appeared with a timid smile as he gestured her inside. "Come in." He was nervous but oddly excited. There were a few moments throughout the day when he half-expected her not to show up. To see her on his doorstep now left him relieved and elated but still wildly anxious.

"Hey, Ben." The words came out rather breathlessly. She realized that she had been holding her breath the entire brisk walk up the stairs. "Oh, I brought you these. I read a few articles that they help." It was then that she remembered the grocery bag that was clutched in her hand. She handed the bag with a box of extra thick condoms to him, and he peeked inside. An immediate, bright red flush rushed to his cheeks.

They had never spoken about their health history before agreeing to have sex with each other. Mari figured that she didn't have much to worry about. She was certain that Ben hadn't been with a woman in quite some time. There was no reason for Ben to be concerned either. Her action over the past few years had only consisted of silicone friends and she was on birth control for the sole purpose of regulating her periods.

"Oh…uh…t-thanks. You must have done the same research I did." He bashfully admitted. "They…may come in handy." As he dropped the bag down to his side, he finally managed to look her in the eye. "I…have to say that I am…thankful for your…discretion and care with the uh…incident. I don't think anyone else would have been quite as…kind or understanding."

Now it was Mari's turn to blush as she dipped her chin demurely. "You don't have to thank me, Ben. We are both still figuring things out. We knew this going in." She shrugged with a shy bit of laughter. "I swear if I had to try this with a new partner, I don't think it would have ever gotten to…um…actually sleep with them. Like…ever."

"Oh…well…too true." Ben nodded in agreement with a soft laugh. "Will you excuse me? There's one thing I have to check on before um…" He awkwardly trailed off as he disappeared into his bedroom. Despite the air conditioning, Mari could feel her perspiration edging towards being uncomfortable. At least that interaction had not gone as badly as it could have. With a quick glance at his door, she tiptoed back over to his bookcase to inscribe her second book.

This peculiar exercise had become cathartic in a way. She quickly signed her name on her second book's title page, along with a brief antidote. Smiling to herself, she closed the book and slid it back onto the shelf. Mari wondered if he would ever bother to open them in the future. If he did, she hoped that he would remember this whole awkwardly hilarious encounter with fondness.

The subtle clearing of his throat startled her, she looked up at him with a breathless smile. That was before she noticed him standing there in a silken robe and she couldn't help but crack up laughing.

"Ben, what are you wearing?" He cast a glance down as if he had already forgotten what he had changed into. The subtle curls of auburn on his chest were peeking out from the V of his navy-blue satin robe. It looked oddly short against his pale legs. She cocked her head a bit to the side in humored wonder. "Why are you wearing a robe?"

"Is a robe not what a man should wear to bed? The articles said that robes were acceptable. Especially silken ones."

"Were you reading Playboy articles by Hugh Hefner? I mean robes are okay, but they should be ones that actually cover your ass." Mari broke into giggles. "I'm pretty sure that's a woman's robe. Where the hell did you get that?"

"The charity shop on the mainland. It's blue I thought it… Does it not cover my…?" Ben reached down and felt along the hemline and his bottom. The immediate blush and surprise on his face gave Mari the only answer she needed. She erupted into further laughter. "Oh. Oh my…"

"Ben it's fine! Honestly you um…won't be wearing it much longer anyway."

"Oh. Um…right…" Ben nodded before he stepped towards his bedroom door with a gesture to Mari. "Well…uh, after you."

Shuffling her way over, she slipped into his bedroom. The flicker of a dozen or so candles and soft instrumental music greeted her at the door. She took in the sight and Ben worried a moment with her hesitation. He thought he needed to explain himself yet again.

"Well…ah…the articles also suggested setting the mood. I…do hope it is to your liking." Mari was touched by the thought and attention to detail Ben had put into their special evening. "I…I-I did not wish for a…um…*repeat* of last time."

"Oh…Ben. This is all quite…lovely." He had gone out of his way to make it a more relaxing atmosphere for the both of them, and she was grateful.

"I am glad you like it. It sounded like a good idea when I read about it. To be honest I gave it a try one night when I-" Ben stopped himself as he was dangerously close to oversharing. He had neglected to explain exactly how much research he and done and what methods he had tried. Including the rather arduous task of learning the complexity described as "edging". He had experimented with that method a few nights. Along with the atmosphere of the candles and low music to see if that helped him at all. "Um…t-to see if it would help me relax."

"Oh well, it always works with me." Smiling softly, she turned to him and reached out to grasp his hand. "I love a candlelit bath with music, and when reading a good book." Ben nodded as he glanced between her and his bed. Unlike last time, he was now anxious to get started. His mind was in the right place. He had spent every day since their last encounter preparing for it. He was ready.

"Would you like to…come to bed with me, Mari?" He whispered in a hesitant cadence as he attempted to ask as seductively as he could muster. Her eyes moved to his in surprise at his outright request and she nodded. With her wordless agreement, he lifted her hand to his lips and kissed her knuckle.

The innocent intimate touch should not have brought an overwhelming wash of heat to her body, but it did. Her mouth went dry as Ben guided her onto his bed. He paused in the middle, on his knees. Mari followed suit.

An odd quiet settled between them as each waited for the other to make a move. Mari hesitated. She had decided to only put on two articles of clothing to speed things along, and Ben was staring at one of them. His gaze was so intense that she felt herself getting overheated. It seemed that the temperature of the room had risen quickly in the short time that they stood there. To avoid a fainting spell, her hands fumbled with her dress. She pulled it up and over her head and she tossed it aside.

Ben's breath hitched as he moved his gaze down her body. He took his time to observe every inch only to realize that she had neglected to wear a bra. He stared wide-eyed at her bare chest. His whole game plan went out the window.

"Ben." The gentle utterance of his name broke his trance. "Please, tell me if I am going too fast." He nodded subtly before moving his eyes back down to her chest. Mari reached out to work on the sash of his robe. She nervously chuckled at his wide-eyed stare at her chest. "You can touch me, Ben." He could only nod in acknowledgment as the robe fell from his shoulders.

"I…would very much like to…" With a strained whisper, his fingers hovered in midair and flexed. Allowing him that moment, Mari took his hesitation to admire him. She wanted to reach out and touch him herself but opted for a more visual appreciation. She didn't want to send him into overdrive just yet.

Little by little he reached out for her. She felt the brush of his fingertips against the swell of her breast. Doing her best to refrain from a reaction so as to not scare him off. Even with the slightest of touches, he was tender and sweet. Ben chanced a subtle caress of her nipple and Mari couldn't keep herself quiet any longer.

"Ben…can I kiss you?" With a slow swallow, his eyes moved back up to hers. He gave her a subtle nod. Mari had meant to make the advance toward him herself, but Ben had beat her to it. His hands cradled her face and brought her mouth to his. It was a kiss that made her melt and left her wanting more.

Mari's arms eased their way around his neck, bringing him in closer, inch by inch. She delighted in the fact that he finally began to relax against her. With a shift of her knees upon the bedding, she eased them both down towards the awaiting pillows. Ben followed her, too entranced with their embrace to think of anything else.

Their kissing continued as she settled into the plush nest of pillows. Ben settled in above her, straddled over her legs. So far, so good. Mari felt confident enough to encourage him some more. Still lost in the kiss, Ben followed her guidance and settled against her body. The weight of his body above provided her an incredible comfort. She slipped a sigh of satisfaction into his mouth.

Ben's hands began to wander across her vacant skin. He was finally ticking off all the right boxes. She again reminded herself to take it slow. That was until his trembling hand fully cupped her nude breast. It made her hips arch up into his. There was a strangled groan as she felt Ben's entire body shudder. She feared the worst.

"I-I-I'm gonna need…a minute…" Their lips reluctantly parted with his breathy plea. The preventative measures that Ben had attempted earlier had not helped him enough. Especially when confronted by a mostly naked woman. He cursed himself for why he hadn't properly trained his body before meeting a woman that he wanted to sleep with.

"Do you want to try what I offered…?"

"I-I…don't want to impose…" Ben moved his gaze back up to hers and looked rather sheepish.

"Ben, it's fine. I offered. I could use the practice." Mari didn't wait for any solid confirmation. She was already pressing him back to the bed so she could climb on top. With her bare breasts so close to his face, his brain completely stalled. It gave Mari enough time to gather her courage to maneuver down his body. To come face to face with the tent in his boxer briefs.

With a quick glance up at him, she sucked in her lower lip and curled her fingers around the elastic waistband. There was a lingering hesitation, but Ben offered no resistance. It was now or never. The curiosity of what he looked like nude outweighed any apprehension she had about moving forward.

Allowing ample space for his erection, she held her breath as she eased the fabric down and over his hips. She couldn't exactly remember the last time she had been that close to a penis. But from what she could recall, Ben's was by far the nicest. Not that she was an aficionado or anything.

She reached out to graze the pad of her pointer finger down his firm length. It offered an intriguing twitch in response. Ben was doing his best to remain calm. But his body couldn't help but writhe against the bedding as his hands strangled the comforter.

Mari shifted and came face-to-face with his manhood. She hovered as she studied the soft and hard contradiction. He could feel the moist heat of her quickened breath with her closeness. She had fallen down the research rabbit hole of oral sex techniques ever since she read that it could help Ben's issue. There may have been a night or two that she stumbled upon some pornographic videos. She wasn't completely into porn, it just happened to assist in her better understanding of the suggested techniques she read about. She was ready to attempt anything to help him ejaculate first, so he didn't have to stress about it. That way they could continue on with foreplay until he was ready and able to go again.

"Ah no…Mari…y-you don't have to-" Ben's shaky words were cut off by his shuddering low moan. She timidly slid her mouth down his length. He tried to keep his hips pressed against the bed, but her mouth felt so incredible. He wanted to thrust himself deeper down her throat. There was little to no train of thought beyond the sensation of the hot wetness of her mouth.

With an experimental suckle, her hand reached out and grasped him below her lips. Despite reading some negative comments on oral sex, Mari found it rather interesting. The noises she was able to effortlessly draw from him urged her on. He hadn't managed to fall apart yet. She chanced letting her mouth and hand work in an uneven tandem up and down his length.

Though inexperienced in the oral sex department, Mari offered more than enough stimulation for Ben. The masturbation session he conducted before she got there had come in handy. If she had attempted this the week prior, he was certain he would have orgasmed from the sheer thought of her mouth. The sensation hit him abruptly. He tried to offer a warning, but his release was beyond his control.

The ejaculate hit the back of her throat unexpectedly. She gagged on the peculiar sensation. Despite her discomfort, she managed to keep her mouth on him until he finally stilled. Gingerly she slid her lips off his length. The release of her mouth from him caused another grunt. Well, at least she managed to get him off. And finally at an appropriate moment.

As she sat up, her tongue moved about in her mouth. She tasted the essence of him, trying to mentally describe the flavor. It was a humored precaution as the subject matter could come up in her novel. Especially if her characters had anything to say about it.

"Oh, bloody fucking hell." Ben gasped out. That was the first time that Mari had ever heard him swear. It was so out of the blue that she couldn't help but snort before dissolving into laughter. At least it managed to break the tension.

She opened her mouth to say some smartass retort, but Ben stalled her effort. He enveloped her lips as he hastily pushed her back down onto the bed. The move surprised her enough to try to pull away from him in question, but his hands held her face fast to his. Mari found herself melting immediately. His kiss was so firm and insistent.

Ben offered no further hesitation as his body blanketed hers. Keeping her pinned, his hands made their way down her body with a sure and questing touch. Every caress pulled the air from her lungs as she felt his hands devouring her by touch alone.

His mouth soon chased after his hands, moving on pure instinct at this point. The sweep of his lips across her skin was lingering. A delightful mix of teeth and tongue left her writhing beneath him. She could feel the warmth of the appreciative sigh against the skin of her breasts. He stopped to pay proper homage to them.

Mari's thoughts raced with a million things all at once. She wanted to say so much, but the words stalled in her throat. There was a fear that any noise might throw Ben off his mission. Mari didn't want to stop him until they both had their fill. That was until he brushed his lips across her nipple.

With a quick bite down on her lower lip, she stalled her noise of pleasure after a brief exhalation. To her relief, it did nothing to hamper Ben's efforts. It only encouraged him to move further down her torso. Underneath his lips, her abdomen sank from the breathy and ticklish kisses. Yet he continued with a murmur of delight. His hands gripped onto the sides of her thighs as his mouth swept over the jut of her hipbone.

There was only one garment of clothing left between the both of them. Mari wanted nothing more than for Ben to rip it completely off of her. His hands hesitated along the elastic. She wondered if he was thinking about the last time. As she went to entice him along, she felt the tips of his fingers curl around the edge as he shimmied the fabric down.

A shuddering sigh slipped from her mouth as the fabric and lace scraped against her flushed skin. For a moment a small part of her hesitated and wondered if Ben was still able to function. He answered her wordlessly after he tossed her underwear aside. His warm hands smoothed their way up the inside of her legs, nudging her open. As she was about to breathe a sigh of relief, he paused.

"Ben…?" Mari whispered out in question as she sat up on her elbows, hoping he only stopped to get ahold of himself. When she glanced down to check on him, his face contorted in a mix of shy confusion. His eyes were locked onto the junction of her thighs.

"I…I must confess… I-I do not exactly know what would be the most pleasurable for you." His gaze flickered up to meet hers. "But I would very much like to."

Mari's mouth went dry as a wildfire broke out beneath her skin. The words were an innocent admission. But the mere fact that he wanted to learn how to please her properly sent her brain into a tizzy. On the one hand, it was delightful to hear. On the other, there was the embarrassment of having to explain her process to another human being. Those dreamy blue eyes looked so desperate and hopeful.

"Ben, you don't have to-"

"I've gotten this far. I should at least attempt to learn how to actually…please a woman." His Adam's apple bobbed with an uneasy swallow as he got the difficult words out. "In every way possible." The words sent a jolt straight to the junction of her thighs. She wanted nothing more than to press her legs together to quell the ache. But Ben's insistent hands kept her spread open.

Her chin bobbed with a slow nod before she laid back down. How the hell does one explain how to please them sexually? Especially to someone who didn't exactly know their way around a woman's body. Achieving her orgasms was always a complicated mix of so many things. Things that even Mari had to take a shot in the dark with sometimes. But then again, she didn't have an attractive man kneeling between her legs during her solo sessions.

"Uh…well…" Her mind raced for the best way to explain it in the simplest of terms. "Kiss me. Down there." She cursed inwardly. That was nowhere near descriptive enough. "But…um…like it's my mouth. Soft and slow…gentle, open-mouthed kisses, with a bit of tongue."

Ben mused over the directions before settling his torso down between her thighs. The moment she felt his warm breath against her moist lips it made her breath catch. Despite all the times before, he did not hesitate as he pressed his warm mouth against her. Mari let out an instant shuddering moan as he had done exactly as she described to him. Except he didn't let up. His mouth continued to press deeper with caressing kisses.

There was a subtle brush of his tongue that happened to catch her clit. Mari was fairly certain she could taste color for the briefest of moments. Her fingers twisted into the bedding, trying anything to remain still against Ben's attempt at oral sex. The touch was so soft and sweet, and she didn't want to chance to scare him off with a buck of her hips. Mari was doing her best to keep her noises of delight restrained, but it made Ben take pause.

"Is this…acceptable?"

"Oh fuck, Ben. Yes!" The enthusiastic answer made his cheeks and manhood flush with excitement. Mari bit her lip to stop the further onslaught of swear words. Something about the learning aspect of this sultry endeavor made him want to continue to absorb as much tutelage as possible. His rapt learning fueled her fire to teach him more. "T-Take your fingers…spread me open." Her breath hitched sharply as he was a bit too probing in his touch. "Gently!"

"S-Sorry…"

"It's okay…that's better…" Mari breathed out. There wasn't exactly an easy way to explain to him how to find her clit, so she reached down to show him. "This…my clit… Just…kiss it, suck it, rub it…just try everything." She teased her bud with a few swirls of her fingers in a demonstration as a sigh fell from her lips. "With your fingers or mouth…or all at once."

Despite the instructions being the bare minimum, Ben demonstrated that he understood the gist of it. With Mari's answering whimpers he knew he was on the right track. The noises he continued to draw from her only encouraged him further. He experimented with different touches to see which would elicit a more explicit reaction. As his mouth suckled upon her, his fingers eased their way further down her slit to trace along her opening. This part he at least had some experience with.

Ben surprised her by easing a finger inside. The answering moan was immediate. Her ache for fulfillment was becoming an insistent need. Emboldened by her response he slid another finger inside. He began to ease out with the withdrawal and smoothly press back. Mari couldn't help the squirm of her behind. His mouth and fingers worked in a slow and delicious tandem.

"P-Palm up…" Mari hoarsely whispered between her sighs. The answering twist of his fingers inside her made her shiver. "Press up, drag your fingers out. Do you feel it? That…rough patch?" Despite Ben's mouth being busy, she felt the subtle shift of his cheek against her thigh as he nodded. "Gently…gently thrust your fingers against that spot…"

Ever the attentive student, he implemented everything that she had taught him. While it was a bit ungainly at first, he found an enticing rhythm that left her speechless. All he needed was some gentle guidance and he was more than willing to apply what he learned. Her noises of pleasure were growing louder and more insistent. Mari found herself heading straight for her peak.

She lost herself to the moment. Threading her fingers through his hair she held onto him tight as she fell into the depths of her delights. Ben hesitated a moment, unsure if he should continue. The rocking of her hips and the delectable moans intoxicated him. The way she pulsed around his fingers made his body ache for hers.

"Ben…holy fuck." Mari panted as she stilled his movements with her hands. "Have you ever made a woman orgasm before? Because…*fuck*." Ben lifted his head up in question.

"So…t-t-that actually was…?"

"It sure as hell fucking was."

Shifting his weight, he sat up and his eyes caught sight of how incredible she looked in her afterglow of bliss. Ben felt himself twitch at the sight and his nails dug into the skin of his thighs where his palms had been resting. The box of condoms on the nightstand drew his attention next.

"So…um…shall we…?"

"Oh…uh…well, if you're okay still…" Ben could only answer her with a curt nod. He had managed to hold himself together throughout his oral sex lesson. That unforgiving ache was seeping into his bones now. He was flushed and ready. It was not bad enough yet that he felt as if he would lose himself immediately. After all they had accomplished that evening, he was determined to see this through.

He ripped the condom box open and pulled one packet from the depths. Mari watched him with quiet nervousness. It was silly to become apprehensive now. He had literally been giving her mouth-to-mouth between her legs only moments ago. Despite the shake in his hands, he managed to roll the condom on.

She took that time to adjust herself more firmly in the middle of a pillow. There was a swift tug of the bedding beneath her as Ben attempted to tuck them in under the sheets. Mari couldn't help but giggle.

His eyes dipped a bit bashfully but oh how his body ached for her. He didn't want to seem eager, but he was finally ready for the final step. There was a rather awkward shuffle of their bodies as he climbed on top of her. Bracing himself on his elbows to either side, his eyes trailed up the line of her jaw to meet her gaze.

Mari smiled softly and reached up to caress his cheek. His body relaxed and she felt his hips shift against hers. There was a mutual hitch of breath as his flushed tip grazed against her folds. A rush of heat radiated out from their point of contact to infiltrate her body.

"Mari..." Ben whispered, almost in wonder. The simple utterance of her name made the entire ordeal more intimate.

"Kiss me, Ben." She insisted, drawing his face down to hers. He obliged with an achingly soft caress of his lips. There was a subtle adjustment of her thighs as she bent her knees to invite him in from pure instinct alone. One hand moved to cradle her hip as he pressed his weight against her before he slid himself inside.

Mari's body went rigid as she felt the fulfilling penetration. There was a long moment where she ceased to breathe. His infiltration was teasingly slow, gritting his teeth to keep his composure. Despite the thick condom, he could feel her envelop him with such eagerness. Even with the influx of new sensations, he was still able to keep his cool as he seated himself inside.

All coherent thought dissipated the moment they became one. Their eyes met as their breaths intermingled and Ben chanced a slow withdrawal. The first few thrusts were slow and inelegant. But with Mari's gentle caresses of encouragement, they found their rhythm in no time.

It was a whirlwind of kisses, heated touches, and whimpers as they lost themselves in one another. There were no lingering apprehensions, no awkwardness. It was only the joining of two humans in the delights of the flesh.

The specialty condoms seemed to help Ben stay focused with calculated thrusts. His basic instinct kicked in, overshadowing all his anxieties and worries. Right now, he wanted nothing more than to feel Mari writhe underneath him. All he could focus on were the noises he was pulling from her and the arch of her hips against his.

"I want to…feel you…orgasm around me…" Ben whispered the broken words against her ear with each slow thrust as he pressed his forehead to hers. A shiver ran down her spine from his accented voice crooning in her ear. Her only reply was a pleading whimper. From the way he was pleasing her, she wasn't going to need much more encouragement.

Her hand slithered between them, reaching down to find her swollen bud. Mari couldn't keep the sounds of delight at bay. She tossed her head back into the depths of the pillow as her entire body arched off the bed. Ben could feel her fingers brushing against the base of his shaft as she teased herself and he shuddered. With the sensations, his hips snapped against hers, increasing their speed and power.

The moan was mutual, and Ben bent down to capture her mouth with his. His hands raked down her body, clutching at her with possessive desperation. Mari cried out into his mouth as she felt it. There it was. That point of no return. That rabid chase towards the epitome of pleasure.

Ripping her hands away from herself, her arms tangled around his neck. Her fingers threaded through his hair, holding onto him for dear life as her orgasm hit her full force. There was an answering guttural groan of bliss as Ben felt her clutch around him with each wave of her peak. That was all it took for him to tumble into the abyss after her.

Chapter Twenty-Three

Mari woke up with a startle.

She was somewhere that she didn't quite know. It wasn't home. That was for sure. Was it the beach apartment? No, it wasn't there either.

A gentle snuffle came from the bed next to her and she froze. Slowly she turned her gaze to the noise. Her eyes went wide as she realized who was sound asleep next to her.

It was Ben.

She was in his bed.

And they were both still naked.

Going into this, she had promised herself that she wouldn't stay over. That's what normal lovers did. She and Ben were not normal lovers. They were platonic friends who happened to agree to have sex for the purpose of scientific study.

His normally well-tamed auburn hair was bed-tousled from the events of the previous evening. She had managed to unleash something. Something that Ben had hesitated with from their last attempt. Last night he had finally managed to succumb.

Oh, and succumb he did. They both did. It was an iconic night of pure human desires. It almost felt…real. As if they had left their insecurities outside the bedroom. That they finally let their instincts take over instead of their usual anxieties.

There was a peculiar urge to slide in closer to him, but no. She couldn't. She wasn't even supposed to sleep over. But what if her characters needed a morning-after scene? How was she going to accurately describe it if she never completely experienced the event herself?

What harm could it do? It was for her book after all. Ben had understood the pretenses so far. This wouldn't change anything.

Ben was handsome though. She couldn't help but stare at him. In his relaxed state, she was able to see the charming kindness in his features instead of only in his actions. There was an attractive effortlessness to him while lost in the throes of sleep. Now if only she could get him to relax all the time instead of in those rare moments on their dates.

One day it would be nice to have every morning be a morning like this one. A lazy morning with no plans to rush off. With strong arms holding her tight. To wake up blissful and warm, next to a man she loved.

Loved?

The thought made her chest seize but she had little time to reflect on the intrusive thought. Ben shifted in his sleep with a subtle stretch as he rolled over on his side to face her. His limp arm flopped over onto her abdomen. The shuffle of his body had kicked down the bedding. It now rested along his lower thigh, leaving most of him exposed to her scrutiny.

In the light of day, she could more easily admire him. She welcomed the distraction away from where her wayward thoughts had gone. He was not muscular but pleasantly toned. She wondered if it was from him toting all those books around in the library. There was a light sprinkling of auburn hair on his chest. She fondly remembered kissing and caressing her way through it the night before.

As her eyes continued to move south, her breathing hitched in surprise. She could see that he was hard for her again. Last night she had managed to coax two orgasms from him and now it looked like he was aching for a third.

Everything had felt incredible. Even though it took a bit of coaxing, she had her first orgasm from penetrative sex. Well…penetrative sex with a human anyway. Her sex toys had managed to give her orgasms countless times. There was a subtle shift of her thighs against each other as she reminisced about the previous night. She rolled onto her back with a sigh to stare at the ceiling.

Mari had no idea that Ben had woken up because of her position change. He had woken up to the view of her lovely profile in the soft light of the morning. Even with the muck of sleep still addling his brain, his thoughts drifted back to the night before. The typical morning anxieties had yet to infiltrate his system. Through hooded lashes he admired her while she was lost in thought. His hand lazily embraced the curve of her side as he slid in closer to her.

Her immediate reaction to his movement was to freeze. But the sweet and tender nuzzle against the crook of her neck defrosted her in an instant. With a languid stretch, his arm hooked around her waist to mold her up against his warm torso. She could do nothing but submit to the welcoming embrace with a soft smile. It was worth getting into her characters' mindset anyway.

"Morning…" Ben's accent was much thicker with the haze of sleep, and she felt her body warm with delight. The resulting fluster caused her to lose her head all over again.

"I'm sorry I-I didn't mean to spend the night…"

Ben tensed ever so slightly as her words broke the amorous spell of the morning. The sigh he released was subtle. He couldn't have cared in the slightest that she had slept there. Their sexual encounter left him delightfully sedated. After that, the last thing he wanted was to spend the rest of the night alone.

Mari had been patient and understanding with him as they took the time to figure things out together. No one before had ever bothered to be that attentive to him. Nor teach him anything in the very few previous sexual interactions. She had given him such an overwhelming boost of self-confidence. It brought a turbulent pool of emotions, and he was having difficulty discerning between them.

"It's alright. I-I don't mind…" Rolling over onto her side brought her nose-to-nose with Ben. Her jaw flexed, not realizing how close he had gotten to her and how it would affect her. There was an overwhelming need to lean in and kiss him. Instead, pure awkwardness spilled from his mouth, and it stopped her short. "So…uh…w-was it good for you?"

Mari didn't want to outright explain to him all he had managed to help her accomplish. So, she settled for a more subtle approach.

"Sure was. You?"

Ben nodded, "Very much."

"Good."

There was a prolonged and uneasy pause before Ben's gaze caught hers. "Can we do it again?"

Mari had to take a moment to process the unexpected request. Sure, Ben sounded like he had enjoyed himself. But she didn't think he would ever want to try something like that again.

"Uh…sure. When?"

"Perhaps…now?"

Innocent desperation was swimming deep within the blue depths of his eyes. That sexual ache within him had returned with a vengeance. Something took over her in that instant and she gave in and kissed him. There was a surprised murmur against her mouth as he hadn't expected her to say yes.

Nothing more needed to be said as they tangled themselves together amongst the sheets. It was a flurry of kisses and heated touches as they both gave in yet again to one another. No more apprehensions, no more worries. To lose oneself in the throes of passion without letting the questioning anxiety overshadow it.

Chapter Twenty-Four

That was all it took.

One night of sex, and the uninhibited morning after, was all it took for Mari to finish writing the rest of her manuscript. She couldn't believe it. That single night and morning after with Ben had fueled her to write over 20,000 words in less than a week. Mentally she was exhausted but physically she was elated. For a whole host of reasons.

Was sex what she needed to encourage such an incredible flow of words? If so, she was cursing herself for not having tried it sooner. Especially during her dreaded writing slumps.

She had taken a few days away from the manuscript before she sent it to a local print shop to print a hard copy. With so many hours of staring at her work on a screen, it was much easier to edit on printed pages. A few days were then spent furiously editing the book. She worked to catch any spelling or grammatical errors. The parts she had trouble with were passages that had been the product of the late-night writing sessions. She typically got a bit carried away with her brain working faster than her typing fingers. There was usually a whole slew of errors.

Within an hour of Mari sending her file over to Faith, her phone buzzed with an incoming call. Mari answered the call but before she could get a word out the tone in Faith's voice caused her to hesitate with her response.

"Are you fucking kidding me, Mari. What the fuck."

"Is it bad…?" The apprehension in her voice matched her wince.

"Okay so I only read a few chapters from where you had left off with the teasers…but you're done? Like, done, done? This huge file is the whole thing? I can't fucking believe it."

"But is it bad?"

"Mari. No. This is *incredible*." Faith's voice had dropped off with breathy disbelief but for only a moment. "Well, from what I read so far. I knew you had it in you. I just knew it. But you're done! And early!"

"I guess the summer at the beach was good for me." She offered as nonchalantly as possible with a nervous laugh.

"Don't ever fucking go home. Seriously."

"Come on, Faith. You've only read maybe a quarter of it. A-And it's my first time attempting true…romance…in my work. It could still be shit for all you know."

Faith outright laughed, "Mari, you just gotta stop being so modest. This could easily be your bestseller ever. I'm going to read the rest of it, even if it takes me all night. I'm already hooked. And fuck knows how many damn books I read every day."

"Well…I'm glad you like it."

"What, that's it? I'm ecstatic to get this sent out to the team. The editors will have a crack at it and then off to the design team to work on a few cover options for you." Mari's head was swimming with everything that came next. Her hard work was complete. But what followed was a hurricane of edits, mock-ups, a release date, pre-orders, marketing, and scheduling a book tour. Only for the cycle to start all over again when she started a new project.

"What? Already? But I thought-"

"Look, the department head peeked at your social media posts. You know, the ones that the marketing team has been posting with teasers of your book you've been sending updates on. The response has been straight-up fire. I think they might even expedite this."

Books cycled through publishing companies. It usually took almost a year to work up the hype and plan the marketing strategy. But since so much time had passed since her last book, they were willing to hurry the process along. With the increasing demand from her fans, the publisher had been hounding Faith. In turn, Faith had been hounding Mari to get a project underway.

"Expedite?"

"In my last roundtable, there was a serious talk about releasing this right before Christmas."

"But that's..." Mari lifted her hand to her face and counted the months down between August and December on her fingers. "Five months from now!"

"Exactly." There was an amused mirth in Faith's tone. "Now do you understand why I'm so fucking stoked you got this finished? It's not even the end of the summer yet!"

"I mean...sure but, that's a lot to consider in such a short time."

"When are you ever going to get it through your thick skull that you are in demand?"

Mari couldn't help her laugh, "Probably never."

"Now you know why I'm getting gray hairs in my 30s. It's all your fault. You're gonna owe me a steak dinner and a cocktail when we meet up for your book tour."

"Fine. Fair enough."

"And one of those top-shelf alcohols, not any of the cheap bullshit."

"You're lucky I like you as my agent," Mari smirked with a sigh.

"So, what's next on the docket? Another romance perhaps?"

"Oh, fuck off."

"Be salty with me all you want, but I know a bestseller when I read one."

Mari leaned back in her chair with exasperation. The last thing she wanted to do right now was think about another idea for a book. She needed to decompress and flush her brain out of any lingering what-ifs about her book so she could move on.

And that included Ben.

Chapter Twenty-Five

The thing about a good thing is that it must always come to an end.

But that was the problem.

She didn't want it to end.

At least she didn't think so.

Her story was now complete and in the hands of her publisher. There was no further need for Ben. Or their arrangement. Their experiment had been a complete and resounding success.

Except every time she thought that she had gathered what courage she needed to serve Ben with a 'Dear John' letter, she couldn't bring herself to do it. She didn't want to do it. She couldn't bear to do it.

Of all the stories she had written, all the characters she had created, why was the relationship between her and Ben something that she couldn't quite figure out? Was it unconventional? Of course. But the whole point of their arrangement had been for them to pretend to date each other. All in an effort to figure out the complexities that were dating in your 30s.

It's not that Ben wasn't nice or attractive, he was very much both. Sure, he was awkward but that's what added to his endearing charm. Any woman would be lucky to have him. That is if Mari had managed to get him past his tongue-tied nonsense. He had improved so much over the summer.

"You're making that look again."

"What?" Mari blinked her way back to the present day and her eyes refocused back on Shannon.

"That *look*."

"I'm not making a look." Reaching out, Mari grabbed her hard cider and took a brisk swig. The pair were chilling on Shannon's large deck in the soft breeze from the ocean. From their seats, they could see a decent sliver of the Atlantic. It was enough of an ocean view for Mari without the need to sit at the beach.

"It's okay, you're still in denial."

"Denial of what? I finished my book. I already sent it off to the publisher."

"I'm not talking about your book, Mari."

"Then what the hell are you getting at?"

"You made that same exact look when Ben came in to get his order today. And you continued to make it the entire ten minutes you talked to him."

"I-"

"Girl, don't deny it. You've got it bad."

"What?" Mari placed her drink back down before bringing her legs up and wrapping her arms around them. She locked them in a secure hold against the onslaught that she knew was incoming. "Ben is...just a friend."

Shannon burst out in an unbridled crack of laughter. "People don't normally sleep with their friends."

"Look, it was for sci-"

Shannon was silent for a second as her face contorted to victorious surprise. "SO, YOU DID! You did! You admit it! You had sex with Ben!"

All the color drained from Mari's face. She hadn't exactly wanted to explain the unusual private arrangement between her and Ben. But her friend always had a way of getting the truth out of her in the heat of the moment. There was no easy way to explain that Mari and Ben's entire setup had been for research purposes. How could she understand that?

"N-No... It wasn't like that-"

"Sure. Sure." Shannon bobbed her head in sarcastic agreement as she downed the rest of her drink. "And I'm the future queen of England."

"We...just wanted to make sure that we...uh...still knew what we were doing..."

"That is the stupidest excuse to have sex I have ever heard. Ben actually fell for that?"

Mari's mouth gaped open and closed a few times like a fish out of water. "H-He suggested it! Technically."

Shannon was taken aback for a moment. "Damn. I thought you were the fucked up one. Turns out you both are. Whatever. You both can be weirdos together."

"We aren't together." Mari dropped her chin and stared at her fingers fussing with the fringe on her cut-off jean shorts. "Besides, Ben doesn't have feelings for me. He did this to benefit himself too."

"So...you have feelings for him."

"Now-what...I didn't say that!"

"Not in so many words. But you are way too easy to read between the lines."

"But...I really don't..." The words trailed off as Mari fell back into her thoughts. What was she missing? What was she doing that was making it so obvious to Shannon to assume that she had feelings for Ben? Maybe she talked about him...a lot. There was always a flutter of her heart waiting for Ben to make his way into the bakery. But that was all because she was good friends with him.

Right?

"Earth to Mari." Shannon waved her hand in front of her friend's eyes with a knowing smirk. "Did you figure it out yet? Or are you still down deep in denial?"

"Are you just teasing me about Ben because you can?" Mari asked with a serious side-eye.

"I mean sure. But mostly because it's so fucking obvious to everyone except you."

"But how is it obvious?!"

"Oh, my sweet, sweet summer child." Shannon reached out to pat her arm in some sort of condescending reassurance. "You give Ben the same look I use to give Luke when he and I first started dating. Sometimes I still do when he's not acting like an ass."

"You're crazy. Just because I look at someone weird, doesn't mean that I like them."

"What about the mere fact that literally everyone at the barbecue believed you were dating? You wouldn't leave Ben's side. I don't think there was even a molecule of oxygen between you both."

"Everyone? Nonsense. I-I…was just…pretending…"

"Girl, that was no pretending like I've ever seen. If that was you pretending, then you need to become an Oscar-winning actress. That bullshit was on point."

All Mari offered was a blank and confused stare back at her friend. Nothing was clicking yet. Sure, she felt the temperature rise whenever he was near her. There had even been all those sweet gestures: the flowers, the coffee, the stuffed unicorn…

"Mari. Be real with me." She pleaded with her friend, relieved to see life back in the glassy stare. "Without thinking, tell me what it's like when you're with Ben.

Really quick, don't even think about it." There was an emphasis on her words with a snap of her fingers.

"Uh...well... I feel...hot. Like gross and sweaty. Nervous? But like...I want to smile?"

Shannon tried to keep her excitement hidden as she continued the interrogation. "Now think about when you're hanging out with me. Or even Luke for that matter. Does the same thing happen?"

"Well, no. That's silly-" Mari immediately dismissed the idea until something registered in her brain mid-sentence. She had always touted that she and Ben were just friends. But Shannon was just a friend too, well her best friend. She had nowhere near the same sort of butterflies in her stomach or lofty smile when they hung out. Shannon sat back and waited for the revelation to cross Mari's face.

Mari hadn't moved forward enough in her current thought process to muse about her feelings toward Ben. She hadn't yet even begun to comprehend the whole actually having sex with Ben part. Because her affinity towards Ben McGregor had happened long before that. That shy smile he always gave made her heart swell. The teases he taunted her with made her skin flush. She had tried to convince herself that he was following the rules of their agreement. She didn't think everything that he did for her would make her actually fall for him.

Mari suddenly realized that she liked Ben.

A lot.

Her bottom lip began to quiver as her gaze flashed up to Shannon's awaiting smug look.

"Is it supposed to feel like I want to throw up and hug him at the same time?!" Mari whined in the midst of her chaotic revelation.

Shannon shrugged nonchalantly, "Pretty much."

"What...? But this feeling is...*awful*."

"Hey, Luke!" His sandy hair came to fruition behind the screen door as he seemed to have apparated out of thin air.

"Yeah, babe?"

"Tell Mari what it felt like to look at me when we first started dating."

Luke cocked a brow in morbid curiosity before he glanced at Mari. The look Shannon shot him, gave him all that he needed to know. The two had spoken at length about the little "arrangement" after Mari had explained it to Shannon.

"Like I wanted to run in the opposite direction and make out with her all at once."

"What? But that makes no sense."

"Mari, love doesn't have to make sense." Shannon piped in.

"What… You think I… There's no way… Not me… I could never…"

Shannon and Luke looked at each other knowingly.

"Mari, you have to tell Ben." Now Luke was fully engaged in the conversation.

"Tell him what?"

"That you love him!" The tone of voice Shannon shared made it seem like it was supposed to be obvious.

"It's only been like what…two months? It's completely improbable to fall in love in that short of a time."

"The saying 'love at first sight' exists for a reason..." Luke reminded her.

"Ben doesn't even like me in that way. This was all a mutually beneficial relationship to him. It's…pointless for you both to suggest otherwise."

"Come on, Mari. We've seen the way he looked at you at the picnic. And that was a month ago already."

"He's always looked at me like he was a lost puppy. Even before he ever uttered one word to me. Besides. He's made it abundantly clear that everything we did was for my book. He was just being nice."

"Maybe you should talk to him-"

"I have. Many times!" An aggravated sigh left her lips as she stood up. "I think you're both delusional. I'm going back to the apartment before either of you completely loses your common sense."

Luke went to open his mouth in further protest but the glare that Shannon shot him stopped him in his tracks. She knew it wasn't worth the further fight. Mari had a stubbornness about her. If she went off and mulled over her thoughts, she would end up seeing the truth. If confronted with the information, no matter how true and proven it was, she would never believe it. She had to arrive at a conclusion on her own.

"Mari?" She stopped with her friend's softer and more solemn tone. "Take my advice or not…but since you finished your book, maybe you should try…another experiment? This time, for yourself." Mari glanced over her shoulder at Shannon. There was a willingness to listen from pure morbid curiosity. Shannon's voice dropped in case Luke continued to listen. "Why not sleep with Ben again? The feeling during and after should tell you all you need to know."

There was a deep flush to her cheeks as Mari stormed off, that far-off look returned back to her gaze. Is this really what love felts like? As if it's some overwhelming sickening elation at any given time? Was it even possible to fall in love in such a short time? There were so many questions swimming about her head. But one question remained at the forefront.

Was she actually in love with Ben McGregor?

Chapter Twenty-Six

Mari had been obsessing over the conversation with Shannon and Luke for days. She managed to elude Ben, but only barely. The island was so small, and she apparently needed a vast amount of room to think. Shannon had given her the space to think, and she was grateful to her friend for that. But only that. Her sage advice and observations only left Mari unsettled. She could not shake the words from her thoughts.

Maybe it would be a good idea for her to go and talk to Ben. Open communication was the best for a healthy relationship. Even a fake one.

Without proper conscious thought, she unwittingly found herself standing in front of Ben's door. The last moment she could recall was walking on the beach in mindless wandering as she tried to formulate her thoughts. She couldn't even remember if she had knocked or not. The clicking of the deadbolt lock answered her question. It brought her to rapt attention as her anxiety took over.

"Mari?" The question was one of surprise.

"Hi, Ben. You're not working now, right?" She recoiled a bit at the stupidity of her current conversation starter. "Right. Of course, you aren't. You're here." The mumbled words were under her breath as she fidgeted on his threshold. It was unlike her to show up completely out of the blue.

"Are...you alright?" The door opened a bit wider as Ben dipped his head down to try to get a gauge on the poor woman. Usually, he was the bumbling fool that always seemed to appear out of nowhere.

"Oh. Me? Yeah, I'm fine. Perfectly fine." Inwardly she cursed herself. There was no way she could play this whole thing cool. Not after her conversation with Shannon and Luke. "Well, no, actually. I um...uh fuck. Well, I am uh...having...trouble with..." *Come on, Mari. Get your shit together.* "Another scene in my book!"

Ben was a bit taken aback by her abruptness. "Oh? W-Well...uh...what seems to be the-uh problem this time?"

"Well, uh. Shit." The curse was quick and under her breath. "I mean...it's another...um, sex scene?" Shannon had told her to go and talk to the man. Not solicit him for sex again.

Ben bristled with a flush at the mention of sex. "A-And...?"

"And I-uh... Well...my um, editor said..." *That's it. Make the perceived issue the editor's fault.* "It needs more...passion."

"...O-Oh."

"Are you free?" Without any ounce of hesitation, Mari slipped past him and into his condo. It was too late to back down now. Ben watched her in surprise as she let herself in. It had been days since he had last seen her. At this point, he was willing to do anything to get her to stay even five minutes.

"I-uh...well yes." The words came out in a flustered jumble as he closed and locked the door.

"Oh good. We can work on this now then." It wasn't exactly a question but more of an enthusiastic demand. Her eyes darted around the room. There was an endless loop of a crackling fireplace video on his tv. An upended book stretched out on the wood coffee table. It accompanied a still-steaming mug of tea. At least she hadn't interrupted anything remotely thrilling.

"N-Now…?" He hadn't expected Mari to show up at his door, let alone to be there to ask him for sex. Every part of him was screaming to give in without a second thought. Having a woman show up asking for sex was almost every man's wet dream. Although with Mari it was the stipulation of it being a part of her writing process for her book.

"Why not? I'm free…you're free." She caressed the breadth of her palm along the back of the leather couch and made her way further into his living room. His heart began to race as he watched the enticing sway of her hips. The floral sundress she wore had the thinnest straps and he wondered if she could even wear a bra with it.

His body was going into overdrive and forcing his hand with his thoughts. Usually, his thoughts were reserved or overly analytical. At this moment they were completely physical. But she wanted passion. All they had been able to accomplish was an inelegant joining that just so happened to get them both off. Was passion even something he was capable of giving her?

Once the fluster had worn off from their initial coupling, he dove head-first into studying additional techniques. He also looked further into the ones she had taught him. Movies, books, magazine articles, and even artwork had found their way into his research. He had also been diligent with keeping up with his self-indulgent exercises. Considering that he had successfully completed sexual intercourse, he was more motivated than ever to perfect his timing and skills. Now here she was finally asking for more and he was ready to give it to her.

Without hesitation.

Ben closed the gap between them in a few effortless strides. Just as Mari was about to question the trepidation, she found herself spun around and pulled against his eager body. All breath left her lungs in an instant as she stood there frozen in shock. The disorientation only lasted a second before she threw her arms around his neck.

Their mouths met in an unbridled hunger. They ungracefully stumbled over each other's feet as they made their way to the bedroom. Backs, elbows, and bottoms were victims against walls and doorways. All in their clumsy approach as they attempted to maneuver blindly down the hall. Neither were even remotely bothered by their journey, not even enough to pull away for a breath of air. They were absorbed in the impossible task of drinking the other in attempted osmosis.

They tumbled down onto the bed. A soft whimper escaped Mari as she felt his weight press her deep into the mattress. There was an endless flurry of hands in their hungry quest to devour the other from touch alone. Ben managed to break their connection, only to move his mouth in suckling caresses down her neck. Gasping for air, Mari keened as she felt the coarse hairs of his beard tickle along her skin. She quickly tossed her glasses onto his nightstand.

Neither of them spared a moment to think. Everything was solely based on frenzied instinct at this point. Which was something both of them needed to delve into. To fully give in to the desires and needs of the flesh without overthinking it.

With a scrape of her nails down his back, she grabbed ahold of the hem of his shirt and dragged it up and over his head. Ben's hand paused her movement so he could remove his glasses and he added them to the nightstand with Mari's. She tossed his shirt into the shaded abyss of the room before she dove back in to recapture his lips.

Ben returned the kiss, lingering a bit longer than he had wanted to as her mouth was so warm and enticing. With Mari distracted for the moment, he wriggled out of his flannel sleep pants. He was bound and determined to answer the question in his mind about what exactly was beneath her dress.

As he broke the kiss, he nuzzled and caressed his way down between the valley of her breasts. He hovered there to await the reveal of her body down by the junction of her thighs. He flushed with heat as he watched her writhe on the bed before him in anticipation. The lingering tease of the slide of the fabric against her skin drew the most delicious of whimpers from her parted lips.

He took only a moment to drink in the sight of her before his mouth followed the rising fabric. There was a delectable mix of deep suckling kisses and brushes of the barest hint of his lips. He was willing to do anything to keep her there. Locked in wild anticipation on the precipice of begging for more. In one fell swoop he shoved the dress up and over her head.

Mari barely allowed him his silent victory. She only let him admire her bare breasts, heaving with her hastened breaths, with a fleeting glance. Her hands reached up and threaded into his hair as she dragged him back to her mouth. Ben took it upon himself to offer her body reverence with his hands instead of his eyes.

Her skin was so warm and smooth beneath his famished hands. He relished in the feel of the soft globe of her breast as it filled his palm. With her answering whimper he swallowed it down as his hands drifted down to the waist of her underwear. They lingered there as his lips drifted to brush across her ear with a breathy whisper.

"Is…is this what you wanted…?" There was a kiss against the lobe. "A moment of passion…" He chanced another kiss beneath her ear. "Where we lose ourselves in one another…?"

All she could offer was a needy whimper of his name. With that acknowledgement, he slid her undergarment down over her hips and over the edge of the bed. Remembering his lesson from before, his hand began its slow ascent up and between her thighs. She ached for him in one place and one place only, but his caresses were giving her everything but. Watching her wriggle in silent need for him made him ache and throb in overwhelming want. At least now he knew he could handle teasing her. He wanted to test his limit.

Mari gasped as she felt the tips of his fingers brush against her folds. She was so slick with desire already. Ben groaned against her collarbone as his hips arched into her thigh. She needed him. Desperately.

With a sudden upheaval, she had Ben flat on his back. She dragged her hands down his torso to curl her fingers into the fabric of his boxer briefs. She wanted to reciprocate the teases but also yearned to have him fill her in one swift thrust. There was a flurry of kisses and touches as she eased the garment down his legs. As he sprang free, she found herself sidetracked. But Ben finished the job by kicking off the offending underwear off his legs.

She eased her hands down the straining heft of him as his entire body shuddered from the intimate attention. As much as she wanted to worship the feeling of him, she wasn't sure how long he would last. There was no way that she would chance it. Not when she was this close to feeling him inside her again.

With a quick shift, she maneuvered her way up his body to distract him with a rapturous kiss. Her hand reached down to position him beneath her as she straddled the width of his body. There was a grace of his hands along her jaw as he held her there as their tongues met.

Lining herself up, she eased herself down the heft of his shaft with a shiver. His fingers almost painfully tangled into her loose hair as he groaned into her mouth. The noise was too delicious to not respond back. With his free hand, he guided her down until he was fully inside her.

The kisses turned more feverous, desperate as the need to move grew to a boiling point. Mari broke the kiss first as she pushed herself up to sit atop him. With a subtle adjustment of her hips, she began to ease herself up and down. Ben latched out to grab ahold of her waist as if it was the only thing on the planet that could ground him to that moment.

Their eyes met in the dim light of the room as they intimately moved together as one. Mari's hands shadowed his, keeping his grip firmly on her. She gradually increased the pace. Their bodies remained locked there in that moment of uninhibited delights. Focused solely on the person before them.

That was when Mari felt it. It was an overwhelming swell and tumble of everything all at once. Feelings and emotions. It felt like a tidal wave crashing over her. Some sort of uncontainable influx of emotions.

Ben's voice broke her trance for a moment as his breath hitched. The curl of his fingers into her skin was almost painful as he neared his peak. Watching him come undone so swiftly beneath her sent her hips into overdrive in a rabid chase for her orgasm.

It built up so quickly that it left her mouth gaping as she cried out, tossing her head back. Ben's moans increased, feeling the grasping spasms of her inner muscles clench around him as she fell off into oblivion.

"Ben…Ben…oh fuck, yes!" Mari cried out as the waves of her climax overtook all coherent thought. "Ben, *I love you…!*"

Ben's eyes flashed open with her exclamation. There was no time to respond as his body simultaneously orgasmed. It hit him with such a brutal force that he cried out with abandon as his hips bucked up against hers. There was an endless stream of moans and whimpers. The two rode out their peaks, seemingly forgetting the confession.

Mari slowed to a stop, gasping for air as she attempted to catch her breath. She felt oddly relieved, in more ways than with just the gratification of her body. The moment of their mutual orgasm had been so intense, almost as if it had gotten her to admit…

Oh no.

Shannon had been right.

But Mari had stupidly gone straight to having sex with Ben instead of talking to him about her feelings. Now she had unabashedly admitted them in the ultimate moment of weakness. All while Ben lay there saying nothing. She needed to get out of there. And fast.

His climax was the strongest one he had ever experienced. Despite that, his brain could only think about Mari's heat-of-the-moment admission on repeat. As if it was a record that continued to skip at that exact moment. It left his brain desperately trying to reboot itself as the hum of his climax still reverberated within him.

The jolt of Mari breaking their bodily connection caused him to only snap out of it a little bit. As much as his brain was screaming at him to say something, or even move, he found that he couldn't. He watched her in a blurred daze as she scrambled to get dressed. Opening his mouth, his tongue felt swollen as he tried to fumble through some semblance of words.

"M-Mari…did you just say-"

"I-I have to go."

Without so much as a glance back at him, she rushed into the other room. Tears began to fall as she grabbed her shoes and purse as she dashed towards the door. Ben had only managed to sit himself up with a reply on the tip of his tongue as he heard his front door slam shut.

Chapter Twenty-Seven

Mari couldn't bear to be on the island any longer.

There was too great of a chance of running into Ben and having to explain her slip of the tongue. Her wildly embarrassing and uncalled-for slip of the tongue. How could she have been that stupid? She couldn't up and leave suddenly without arising suspicion among multiple people. She had to make a careful exit all while avoiding Ben and the conversation it would bring.

She wouldn't dare face him. Not when he didn't reciprocate her feelings. It was a stupid Freudian slip in the heat of the moment that she didn't think she would ever recover from. The last thing she wanted was needing to explain herself. And all the awkwardness.

It was easier and safer to pack up and leave. She had gotten her fill of the Jersey shore with her prolonged stay. Every hour she lingered in her limbo of thoughts she grew more antsy to get out of there and back home where it was safe. Safe from the prying eyes and probing questions from Shannon and Ben.

As much as it killed her to not stop and say her usual proper goodbyes to her friend, it was for the best. If Shannon caught even a glimpse of her tortured look, Mari was certain she would crumble. That she would crumble and let her onslaught of feelings tumble out into a heaping pile at her feet. Sending her a goodbye text was the least painful option. Without further torturous thought, she packed up her stuff and left for home.

Ben had gradually become more concerned as the days continued on with no sign of Mari. No familiar and welcoming face at the bakery. He didn't exactly want to pry Shannon for her whereabouts. For all he knew, Mari was locked up in the apartment writing furiously once again. The bakery always seemed like it had ample help and Shannon never looked concerned. He had even chanced to stop by the apartment a few nights after work. But he always found it dark, and his knocks went unanswered.

Now it was a week before the start of September and the Labor Day holiday weekend. The need to seek Mari out had hit a crescendo. There were so many questions swimming about in his head. Namely, the second-to-last thing she had ever said to him. That she loved him.

For days he swore that he misheard her. She had stormed out before he had even managed to utter a proper question in response. He had been in a post-coital daze. Hardly able to rub two brain cells together, let alone process those three little words that had left such an impact on him. But as he continued to replay the scene in his head and her response, he was so sure that she had indeed said it.

"Hey, Ben. The usual today?" Shannon looked up from the tray that she was pulling from the display case with a smile.

"Well…no, actually." Wringing his hands together, he attempted to assemble some coherent structure of words in his agitated state. "H-Have you seen Mari?"

Shannon stood up with her brow furrowed in question as she stacked the tray atop the four others on the counter behind her. "Mari? Mari left two weeks ago, Ben." Wiping her hands on her apron she stepped up to the front counter as her face switched to that of concern. "She told me that she had let you know that she was leaving. She finished writing her book."

"S-She did?"

"Did she not text you?"

"Oh…well-"

"Have you…even *talked* to her…?"

The conversation made Shannon more suspicious by the second. Mari should have gone over to talk to him after she and Luke had confronted her about her feelings. Instead, she had avoided him and the entire situation once again. Ben dropped his chin as disappointment shadowed his features.

"No."

"Fucking Mari." Shannon huffed under her breath as she shook her head in disappointment. From his answer alone she was sure that Mari hadn't even bothered to talk to Ben after the little intervention. "Well…she said that her publisher was expediting her book to print. So, she needed to be back home to coordinate all the chaos.

"Oh." Ben paused as his eyes fixated on a chip in the bakery's countertop. "That makes sense." His voice was almost monotone as his brain drifted off into a chaos of thoughts. "Um…thanks, Shannon."

"You good, Ben?"

"Yeah…I'm just glad she…finished her project. She had been…so stressed and all over it." Ben didn't have to utter his disappointment. It was evident in the slow cadence of his voice. Shannon felt her heart sink as he slipped her a small smile with a nod in thanks. "Thanks, Shannon. I suppose...I'll see you later."

Squinting from behind his glasses, he walked back out into the bright sunlight of the August afternoon. Despite the warm day, he felt the chilling numbness run down his spine. How could she just up and leave? Especially after all that? To use him and his body for the purpose of writing her book.

It should have made him inherently angry. Angry enough to want to write her off for good, to never think of her again. The anger would be pointless. The point of their dating exercise was a mutual learning opportunity. It was never meant to be real.

But it felt real. The feelings had become real. Real and all-encompassing. Enough so that it was all he could think about.

With her heat-of-the-moment confession, he had been obsessively thinking about his own feelings. Neither of them ever discussed what should happen had they ever ended up developing them. She was a reclusive author, and he didn't expect anything from her, aside from their already-agreed-on terms. The last thing he had ever expected was to actually develop feelings for her.

Mari was funny, charming, and a good conversationalist. She had a brilliant mind that was constantly analyzing human interactions. She was just as awkward as himself. But she never minded his nonsense. In fact, she almost made him feel like it was endearing.

There was no way he could go running after her based on maybe a blurted-out exclamation. Something that could have easily happened in the heat of the moment to anyone. The words could be completely meaningless. But why couldn't he get them or Mari out of his head?

Chapter Twenty-Eight

The nonsense needed to end now.

All summer Shannon had been caught in the middle of the weird push and pull between Mari and Ben. Now it was the beginning of December, and their connection was still vastly evident. While it had started off sweet and oddly adorable, it turned into something beyond frustrating. They were two well-educated adults. One wrote about human nature for a living while the other read about it. Yet neither of them had been able to figure out that their little pretend dating pretense had blossomed into so much more.

As was tradition, Mari had sent Shannon an advance reader copy of her new book. Shannon was always delighted to support her friend and offer her feedback and whatnot. Mari's talents were beyond her capacity. She felt like she could barely offer a decent critique because her work was that good. Even if it was a subject matter or genre that Shannon had no interest in, Mari had the talent to suck her into the story. Except this book was beyond the exception.

Mari's new book left Shannon *seething*.

It offered countless laugh-out-loud moments from the adorable dorkiness of the main characters. But there were also sweet tears of sadness and, thankfully, happiness all wrapped up in the simple pages of a book. What she had discovered was what she had always suspected. Because the bullshit she had just read answered all her questions about what had gone on between Ben and Mari all summer. It was obvious to Shannon but completely oblivious to anyone else who happened to read it.

Except for Ben.

Knowingly or unknowingly, Mari had written a public love letter to Ben. Her new book was going to be an instant hit. It was so sweet and tender with such down-to-earth humor but a blossoming love story at the very core of it. Shannon had stayed up to an ungodly hour the past few nights to finish it.

Shannon had sent her friend countless texts with updates and commentary on the story as she read through it. Only for each of them to go unanswered. Mari hadn't even left Shannon on read. She had completely ignored her. It might have been due to the fact that almost every text she had sent said something along the lines of:

I WAS RIGHT

If Mari was going to play that game, then so was Shannon. She was always ready for a little hardball. Especially for the well-being of her best friend. Even if Mari didn't know that it was all in her best interest. Mari had always been a stubborn recluse. She never had a high opinion of herself, despite her talents and being a wonderful person. Now happiness and contentment were literally staring Mari in the face. She was either stupidly oblivious to it or ignoring it. Since Mari wasn't going to talk to her, then Shannon needed to get Ben involved.

Poor sweet Ben. She couldn't help but feel sorry for him. But he was being as ignorant or in as deep of denial as Mari. Maybe even more so. At least Shannon had gotten Mari to somewhat admit that she felt something for the librarian. Now it was Ben's turn. She hoped she could make it to the library before he locked up for the day.

The chime on the library's door rang cheerily. Which was unlike the look on Shannon's face as she stormed through the entrance. She was on a determined mission to confront Ben once and for all. From their conversation weeks before, Shannon was certain that Mari hadn't bothered to send a copy to Ben. He needed to know, even if Mari stupidly wanted to keep it from him.

"Hi, Shannon." Ben glanced up from the book he was reading at the front desk with a smile. It immediately flatlined as he saw a wild mix of chaos swimming in her features. She looked half-crazed and ready to burst or start a fight. Or both. "A-Are…you alright?"

Without saying a word, Shannon slapped a book down onto the counter. His ocean-blue gaze hesitated a moment but dropped to it in curiosity. It looked like one of the other dozen or so books the library had. With fun cartoon-like art on the cover that was eye-catching. But his heart seized when he noticed the male and female characters. They looked suspiciously like him and Mari. Noting Mari's name on the cover, his gaze shot back up to Shannon's.

"You *need* to read this." Shannon firmly put her pointer finger down on the cover. "This…this fucking bullshit." Ben bristled at her firm tone as she shoved the book across the counter to him. "I don't know what the hell happened between you both, but you need to put it back right again. Or…just make it right in the first place! Without all this fake pretense nonsense…or whatever *nonsense* you both agreed to!"

His mouth gaped open with question, but he couldn't find the words to ask them. Shannon was ramming a thousand things down his throat all at once. He had no idea that she had even known about his and Mari's private arrangement. Which only made this sudden confrontation all the more uncomfortable.

"Her book release is tomorrow. She'll be in New York City for the launch at the bookstore in Times Square." Her face finally softened as her eyes turned to a silent plea for her friend. "If you care about Mari, even in the least bit, you'll go. Especially after reading this book."

With that she turned on her heel and left, leaving the book and a stunned Ben behind at the counter. Since Mari had left, the days had passed by in a wordless blur. Despite the change in season and the growing chill in the air, Ben's mind had been stuck in the depths of the summer. His thoughts were still of Mari. Every day he came to work and looked over to the table that used to be her home base for writing her book. The thoughts still lingered when he went home at night, and he attempted to sleep in the same bed that they had been intimate in.

Everything that she had taught him over those months was still ever-present in his brain. Perhaps there was a small part of him that still waited for her to come bursting through the library doors. Coming in with that same distraught look with another book idea that she needed to finish. It had been wishful thinking on his part.

His eyes moved back to the book before he gingerly picked it up to study it. *Romancing the Pages*. It even sounded like a book-themed romance. From what he recalled from earlier conversations; her publisher had only asked her to add a little bit more romance to her books. Not actually write a full-fledged contemporary romance novel.

Flipping through the book, his eyes landed on the dedication page at the front. There was an electric jolt straight to his chest. He lost all semblance of breathing as he read the inscription:

> *To the awkward librarian who stole my heart.*
> *Thank you for showing me that finding happiness with someone is possible.*

There was no denying it now.

Mari's words had been real, whether she had wanted them to be or not.

Ben cursed at his stupidity. Her admission had left him stunned and frozen on the spot. Why did he sit there as she ran off? He should have had the balls to go after her that night. Even if he would have had to run out of his condo completely naked.

It was an unspoken blessing that Shannon had arrived minutes before closing. Ben rushed through the closing procedures. He needed to get home immediately and read Mari's new book. The inscription had opened up a door that he didn't know existed. Or was it one that he had hoped for?

With one final pull on the front door to assure it was locked, he turned and rushed to his car. Based on Shannon's stark review, her book was something that he needed to study in-depth. Immediately.

Chapter Twenty-Nine

Ben didn't bother with putting his bag and shoes in their regular proper place when he walked in the door to his condo. They were carelessly discarded by the door as he was already four pages into Mari's new book. As soon as he had grabbed his stuff from the car, he opened the book to page one. He began to read it during his ascent up the exterior stairs to his second-floor condo on the bay side of the island.

Within only a few pages, he was thoroughly engrossed. Like all her other books, it drew him in so much that he lost track of the outside world. It was some time before he realized that he was still wearing his shoes. As he scrunched down into his recliner a bit more, he kicked off his loafers and moved on to the next chapter.

Every word in the story was an odd mix of a soothing balm of pleasant but awkward memories. Memories that had clearly been influenced by his and Mari's experiences over the summer. It felt like the story had been written as some sort of complex written mental therapy. As if Mari needed to write down her thoughts and feelings to further process them.

Her words were lovely, and the story had him completely entranced. He was finally in Mari's mind from over the summer, watching their relationship from Mari's eyes as the female character fell in love. There was a constant reluctance with the main character that he found solace in. An odd sort of relief washed over him. Mari had been in the same exact mental and emotional struggle as he.

The both of them had been too reluctant to come to terms with the fact that maybe the other felt the same way. Or at least had some semblance of feelings that could turn into something very real. Neither of them had the best relationship background. Most of the time the feelings were not reciprocated, not even in the least bit.

He never tore his eyes from the book as he helped himself to dinner. He ate as he stood, hunched over the small island with the book spread open by his fingers. From there he moved to stretch out on the sofa until the hour grew late. The book followed him to the bathroom as he readied himself for bed. Even as he brushed his teeth the book never closed. He had to coordinate a complex maneuver with his elbow to keep the book open as he put toothpaste on his toothbrush.

The only time he managed to take a small break was to change into his t-shirt and pajama bottoms to sleep. It was less than a minute before his nose was back in the book. He knew if he laid down, he would fall asleep with the rhythmic lull of his eyes darting back and forth across each page. Instead, he wandered back into the brightness of his living room and began to pace in front of his couch.

It was well past midnight when he felt the ache in his cheeks. Reaching up he rubbed his skin through the scruff of his beard only to realize that he had been stuck smiling. For someone who had never delved head-first into romance, Mari had hit it completely out of the park. There was something so genuine, so raw, and realistic about her story. Perhaps it was because he had lived it himself.

Dropping the book on the couch, he collapsed down onto the leather cushion with a loaded sigh. He removed his glasses and rubbed the heels of his hands into his eyes. It was a desperate attempt to rid them of the dry haze that had set in from the endless hours of reading. Despite the late hour, he was restless. His mind was swimming with everything he had absorbed from the book.

More than anything he wished that Mari was still on the island. Even with it being the middle of the night, he would have marched right up those apartment steps. The instant she would open the door he would grab onto her and kiss her. He wanted to show her that she shouldn't have been so afraid of those words.

Putting his glasses back on, he rose from the couch and wandered over to his bookshelf. Deep in thought, his blue eyes darted along the titles of the carefully curated collection. They paused on Mari's small set of books. He smiled to himself as he fingered the spine of her first book. He remembered that the critics all raved about the up-and-coming young author. Being a librarian, he was reluctant to jump on the latest book trends. He had eventually relented and finally understood what all the fuss had been about. If only he had known then that he would be pining for her years later. Ready to fully confess the overwhelming feelings he had for her.

His finger cocked the book forward and into his awaiting palm. From what he could remember from her first book, Mari's new book was significantly more emotionally elevated. Even though it wasn't in the same genre, there was still an elegance about it. It still had her unique style to it.

Flipping through the book, he was hit by the crisp smell of the ink on paper. It wafted up to him and sent a few of his auburn strands shuffling about. Something caught his eye on the title page, and he quickly sped back through the pages to find it. Scrawled in the bright blue pen was Mari's artful signature and an inscription. She had somehow managed to sign the books during one of her visits to his condo.

A subtle smile curled at his lips as the pads of his fingers traced over her signature. He froze as he read the written inscription:

To Ben,
Thank you for the summer of awkward adventures.
I will always have fond memories of you and what you shared with me.

He stood there in a daze for a long moment before he snapped the book closed and shelved it. Now he was curious. Did she manage to sign the rest? Picking up her next book, he shoved the first few pages aside to the title page to find another inscription:

Ben,
No matter what happens between us, this summer has been the greatest experience of my life.
But I hope it never ends.

Ben's heart was racing at this point. As he shoved the next book back onto the shelf, he simultaneously plucked the last book up and opened it. And like the other two before it, this one also had an inscription:

My dearest Ben,
I don't think I could ever thank you for what you've done for me. You've given me hope that love really is out there. Maybe even with you.
Maybe one day you'll read this and laugh or maybe one day this book will sit on our bookshelf.

As tears welled in his eyes, he snapped the book closed before blindly sliding it back on the shelf with the others. Turning on his heel, he walked in the direction of his bathroom. He didn't care what time it was, he needed to get ready to leave for New York. There was no way he was going to miss another opportunity to run after her.

Chapter Thirty

The mid-December morning broke brisk and cold. Despite the weather, there was already a long line waiting outside of the bookstore when Mari arrived early for her book signing. The critics and advance readers had already spoken. Her book was going to be an undeniable sensation. It seemed that they did not care that it was outside of the usual genre and base story. Based on the growing crowd outside, it didn't seem that her faithful fans cared either.

Part of her was elated to see such a warm welcome for her newest creation. While there was another that was crestfallen with the chain of events that had occurred for her to write such a book. Not a day went by that she didn't think of Ben. Some small part of her had looked out her window every day. Waiting for him to show up on her doorstep and confess his feelings to her. Months later it was a daydream in a fantasy.

All those romance movies that she had ended up watching in the wake of her completing her book had been a lie. The guy always ran after the girl in some either wildly romantic or awfully inelegant way. But Ben didn't feel that way about her. She had to keep reminding herself of that. Their entire arrangement had been, for the most part, offering her fodder to write more romance into a book. Not to fall in love.

Despite all the time they spent together, and all the dates, not once did either admit to the other that there were true feelings afoot. Maybe it was the denial that, despite their fake pretenses, there was something very real there. There had been so many opportunities for her to say something to Ben. Instead, she dropped a bombshell on him in the middle of an intimate moment. Then ran away like the coward that she was. Although she had assumed that it had been for the best since Ben did not come after her. He must not have felt the same way. Which was fine with her. At least she thought it was.

Mari tried not to dwell on her thoughts of Ben. Which was difficult considering the book tour she was about to embark on was for a book that was inspired by him. Shannon had arrived the night before to be by her friend's side and was a welcomed distraction. It was tradition for the pair to have a sleepover before a book release. Mari was always nervous. Her friend seemed to be the only thing that could calm her enough to at least manage some sleep. She even helped with the mental preparation for meeting the growing number of fans.

This book signing was going to be much worse for a whole number of other reasons other than the endless throngs of fans. There was a request to be in the public spotlight. Some bookstores were offering a Q&A along with the book signing. Sure, it meant more money in her pocket, but she knew what the number one question would be. "What inspired you to write this book that's so different from all your others?" Mari had rehearsed a thousand different explanations, all of which seemed so inauthentic. She didn't have the heart to tell the world that it was an awkwardly charming beach town librarian who had unknowingly captured her heart. With a cliché fake dating trope.

For someone who had avoided romance for most of her adult life, she sure walked right into it. Willingly no less. A real-life, mainstream, contemporary romance. Unfortunately, it had all been one-sided.

Sitting further back in her seat, she hid from the curious eyes of those waiting in line. The large black SUV turned down the side street to the employee entrance of the bookstore. Despite the excitement of the day, it was still relatively early and those in the car were quiet. Mari knew she was in desperate need of more caffeine and hopefully, they could keep it coming. It was odd to have Shannon remain so quiet. Usually, she was the hype person for Mari.

The SUV slowed to a stop and Faith patted Mari's thigh to bring her back to the current task at hand. Snapping back to the present, she nodded and opened the car door, Faith scooting out right after her. The bookstore staff was quick to offer her a warm greeting as they ushered her in through the side entrance. Shannon followed after, as she had been sitting in the third-row seating. She lingered outside, looking at the crowd. Mari only dwelled on it for a moment as she hurried inside and out of the chill.

Faith and the publishing team had outdone themselves with the preparations. There was such beautifully designed signage in the window and to either side of her table. They accompanied an eye-catching balloon arch stemming from swirled columns of her stacked books. It was quite the photo op if she ever saw one. All the pomp and circumstance reminded Mari that the press would be there. Depending on how her book did on the bestseller list, there would be interviews to schedule between her tour stops as well.

"Even though I hate all this nonsense..." Mari leaned in towards Faith. "This does look pretty fucking fantastic." Faith grinned with a teasing elbow to the author's side.

"If you couldn't tell yet...everyone is psyched. Did you even see the line outside? It's insane!"

"Yeah...don't remind me. I just want to get through this without having a damn anxiety attack from people overload."

"Fair enough. Maybe you'll change your mind when you hear people gushing about your book." The two halted their conversation as the store manager wandered over looking rather elated, despite the early hour.

"Good morning Ms. Quay. We have you all set up for the event. Would you care for any refreshments?"

"Yes!" Mari said loudly and more desperate than she had meant. "I mean...yes, please. Large caramel latte with an extra shot of espresso." The woman turned to Faith and Shannon for their orders before disappearing off to the coffee bar. Mari meandered over to the table to take in the view. Even though this was not her first book success, it was still so surreal to see her name advertised. More so when she remembered that there was an entire line of people bursting with excitement to meet her.

"Well...you did it," Shannon whispered to her over her shoulder with a soft smile. "Kind of worth hanging out at the beach all summer with me, huh?"

Mari laughed but there wasn't much mirth to it. "Well...I'll let you know when the numbers come in." There was a pause as her mind yet again drifted to thoughts of Ben. "But yeah...despite the awkwardness...it's a summer I will never forget." Leaning in, Shannon wrapped her arms around her friend in a reassuring hug. She hoped that her come-to-God moment with Ben had paid off and he was waiting outside with the rest of the fans.

The store manager wandered back, expertly manhandling the three drinks. An employee followed behind her with a small tray of muffins, bagels, and fruit cups for the trio as the staff finished the setup.

"I do apologize that we aren't quite ready yet." She carefully placed the cups down on the uncovered side table where the staff was still unloading books. Mari eagerly reached out and brought the cup to her lips. "We had a lot more pre-orders than we anticipated!" There was a strangled noise as Mari fumbled with her coffee. Faith shot her a look as her brows almost disappeared into her hairline.

"Hell, Mari. I told you that romance was hot right now!"

"Yeah, but...*holy shit*." As bad as Mari had needed her caffeine boost that morning, her coffee remained untouched. Shannon wriggled excitedly next to her.

"Guess I'm going to get my workout by passing those books to you!"

"You sure you're up for this nonsense?" Mari joked as she reached down to clasp her friend's hand.

"You know it. No matter what, I'll always be cheering for you." Shannon slipped her a reassuring smile before it turned into a playful smirk. "Well...until you do something stupid, and I have to smack you upside the head. You're lucky I haven't done it yet. For *many* reasons."

Mari swatted at her arm and gave her hand a rough squeeze before admitting defeat with a heavy sigh. "Look, I told you. He doesn't feel that way about me. Besides, it's been months. If he wanted to actually be with me, he would have done something already." Her words were strong but the tone behind them was anything but. "It's fine though. I'm thankful for what we had. What we did. I don't regret it for a second. I mean...look where it got me."

Shannon gazed at her friend and kept her mouth shut. Despite having so much to say, she knew it wasn't worth it. Not at this moment anyway. All she could do was hope and pray for Ben to show up. If he knew what was good for him. And Mari.

The trio settled as they watched cart after cart roll in and unloaded next to the signing table. Mari managed to nibble on a plain bagel as she nervously sipped her latte. Part of her regretted this endeavor. She had never anticipated such an outcome when she was cornered earlier in the year to write her book. Yet the journey to get to that point was something that she would never trade for. Awkwardness and all.

"Ten minutes to go…" Faith glanced down at her watch as she disposed of her coffee cup. "Better assume the positions." Shannon gave Mari's shoulder a reassuring squeeze as she took up her usual post as the book passer. It was such a small thing, but she loved being able to support her friend as her somewhat adopted family. Faith was hovering about, making sure that the table looked up to her standards. She had mentioned that some of the bigwigs from the publishing company were going to stop by that morning to partake in the excitement.

Despite the massive surge of people outside, the bookstore staff was organized and ready for the onslaught. It was the "it" bookstore for high-profile authors to come in and do book signings. This was a regular occurrence for them to set up and deal with. So when they opened the doors, there was no mass exodus toward her table. It was an orderly fashion. The fans handed in their tickets and followed the roped-off area towards Mari and her mountain of *Romancing the Pages* books.

Mari quickly got over her anxiety as she soon realized that a lot of the fans were even more nervous than her.

Signing books had become second nature and she easily fell back into the rhythm. Everyone was so kind and sweet. A few fans even dropped a gush of compliments in the few seconds they had with her as she signed their book.

Faith hovered by her side. Her own nerves had set in as the executives were due any minute. Mari was unperturbed as she was the one making them plenty of money and doing her due diligence as a contracted author. But it was amusing to watch Faith sweat it out for once.

Once they did arrive, Mari was thankful for the signing break as Faith offered up introductions. The group offered their congratulations. They were quite satisfied with the outcome of the months of Faith's nagging. The small talk quickly grew tedious, and Mari took her leave to sit back down to sign more books. A crackle of a newspaper caught her ears followed by distant excited murmurs from Faith.

"Mari." There was a crack in Faith's voice that caused Mari to look up at her in question. She shuffled back over to Mari's side. Before Faith could continue, Mari turned back to finish signing the current book in front of her. "You did it. Holy shit you really did it."

"Did what?" With a warm smile, Mari slid the book back across the table to the fan before turning in her seat to face Faith head-on. The newspaper was being strangled in Faith's hands as she struggled to contain her excitement. Faith turned to the crowd and projected her voice with a grin over the hum.

"Thanks to everyone here," The crowd hushed, and Faith took a moment to enjoy the dramatic pause. "Mari's book debuted at number one on the bestseller list!" A look of shock fell over Mari's face. She popped up from her chair as if it had turned into a bed of prickly needles and turned towards her agent. The words had hit her but hadn't completely sunk in yet. There was a resounding cheer with clapping from the fans waiting in line. Despite the noise in the building, all Mari could hear was the blood rushing through her ears.

Faith closed the gap between them and offered a warm hug. "Congratulations, Mari! After this, we are so fucking celebrating! I don't care if I have to order room service and we eat it in our pajamas. This is incredible!" Mari beamed as a flush of color blossomed on her cheeks. Perhaps a home at the shore was a very real pipe dream after all.

The cheering had finally died down and Mari collapsed back into her seat with a breathless smile. As much as she wanted another break to rest her hand, the quicker she got through the book signing, the quicker she could get back to her hotel room. She knew she was going to have to decompress from all the excitement of the day. Faith laid out the newspaper on the table next to her with another excited squeal.

She couldn't believe it. It was there, in actual print, and she couldn't believe it. *Romancing the Pages* by Mari Quay had hit the number one national bestseller status even before it officially went on the market. In a daze and still staring at the paper, she reached out with her hand to beckon the next fan forward.

The familiar suede finish of the heft of her book hit her hand and she brought it down onto the table. She opened the book up to the title page as if it was a reflex.

"What would you like the inscription to be?" There was an odd silence before a subtle clearing of a throat.

"I love you too."

The words hit her with a shock straight to her heart. She sat frozen for a moment as her brain calculated if she had hallucinated. With her hands still clutching the pen and the book, she lifted her chin up ever so slowly. Her eyes locked onto the familiar and tender gaze of sweet cerulean blue behind tortoiseshell glasses.

It was Ben.

There he was, looking a bit forlorn but seemingly bursting at the seams. There was a shadow of exhaustion under his eyes, but despite that they sparkled back at her. His collared shirt was untucked and a bit wrinkled from his hasty overnight drive up to the city. As he had learned from their summer dating lessons, a lush bouquet of a dozen red roses and greenery awaited her.

There was no hesitation this time. She dropped the pen on the table and hastily stood. Had she been a bit more agile, she would have dove across the table to get to him. Instead, she opted for a hurried half-skip around the table. Launching herself at him, she encircled her arms around his neck as she pulled him in for a rapturous kiss.

Ben bristled with the onslaught of the warm welcome in front of the large crowd. There was only a breath of hesitation before he wrapped his arms around her back. The bouquet's paper wrapping crinkled as he crushed her against him. Even though months had passed, that now unmistakable spark electrified the connection between the both of them.

"I-I can't believe you're here." Her eyes flitted across his face as her hands caressed the scruff on his cheeks in wonderment. "I-I was so sure after what I said…t-that I had scared you off. *For good.*"

"Scared me off?" He blinked down at her in surprise. "I spent all those weeks in denial because…I didn't think you felt the way that I did. I-I knew it was all pretend…but I couldn't help it…" Ben desperately tried to find the right words to put together as he pulled her closer. "But I fell. For you. I fell for you" He grimaced with the inelegance of his explanation. With a sigh, he took a moment to recollect his thoughts. "After the summer we had…and what you inscribed in all your books to me…how could I stay away?" There was a tender brush of fingertips as he caressed her cheek.

"You took your sweet ass time." Mari teased as her fingers played with the hair on the back of his neck.

"Now that, that was your fault. Because well-uh…apparently the master writer needed her space as she's the one who left me high and dry." Mari narrowed her eyes at him but let him continue. With a quick gesture of his head, he nodded in the direction of her mountain of books. "And look what happened." Mari couldn't help but return his smile. "So…a bestseller, huh?" Ben murmured with a lop-sided grin as he touched his forehead to Mari's.

"Apparently, yeah."

"Maybe you can celebrate properly with this awkward librarian later. I believe I did inspire the story after all…"

Mari giggled with a quick scrunch to her shoulders as she pulled him in for another kiss.

"Ben…are you asking me out?"

"I do believe that I am asking, the woman I love, out on a *real* date."

"I thought you'd never ask."

Epilogue

Two summers later…

A lovely breeze wafted in through the open French doors of the third-floor balcony. It was soft and worshiping as the salty air caressed her skin, leaving goosebumps in its wake. Mari glanced up at the gauzy curtains billowing out and she admired their graceful movement for a moment.

She was deep in the trenches of writing yet another romance book. Although at this point, she had lost count of how many projects she was juggling. The words had been flowing out from her brain, through her fingers, and onto the keyboard of her laptop. Three books were already in various stages of publication with her more-than-pleased publisher. Two additional books had been published since and they had as warm a welcome as *Romancing the Pages* did with her fans. The calls with Faith turned into more of a friendly monthly catchup. Instead of a stressful hounding for more book ideas.

The day of the book's release was cemented in her memory. Her mind often drifted back to the excitement. After her and Ben's share of kisses in front of the large audience of captivated fans, she felt that she owed the crowd some sort of an explanation. She introduced everyone to Ben as being the muse for her book. He had received a resounding cheer and Faith looked like she was about to collapse from the sheer shock. Even though she had embarrassed him with the public introduction, Ben stayed by her side through the rest of the book signing.

Despite the elation of her book debuting at number one on the bestseller list, Mari had cut the festivities short with her team and opted for an early night in. She didn't have to say anything to Shannon. She had shot Mari a look with a resounding wink before Ben dragged her up to her hotel room. The night was spent, naked, in his arms, succumbing to the passion they had tip-toed around for months.

The two of them were finally free of the pretenses and could admit their feelings for each other. There had been seemingly endless heated admissions of "I love you". Unlike before, this time they were returned and repeated throughout the passions of the night.

The story behind Mari's book was too juicy not to share. With the public kiss and admission, the requests for interviews came flooding in. It only added to the pandemonium surrounding the release. Sales continued to climb, and more cities were added to the book tour. With each new added stop, she felt increasingly more confident and excited. Especially with Ben at her side supporting the story they had both created together.

The room grew quiet without the incessant clacking of her keyboard. She could hear the dull roar of the ocean waves just over the dunes. With the unbridled success of her *Romancing the Pages* book, Mari had been able to build the beach house of her dreams. It was right on the oceanfront of Seven Mile Isle, on the outskirts of Avalon. Her dislike for sand lessened quite a bit as she now enjoyed her daily walks along the water in all sorts of weather.

"Should I close the window, Mrs. McGregor?" Ben's crooning accented voice sounded behind her as he lovingly draped a throw blanket along her shoulders. Mari smiled and glanced up behind her as her hands found his.

Most of Ben's days off were spent in his leather recliner next to the floor-to-ceiling bookshelves in Mari's office. She welcomed his warm presence as she worked. He usually sat in silence, reading one of the many books from their growing collection.

"I rather like the sea air." Her eyes turned back to her laptop screen that was awaiting her continued attention. "You know how it inspires me."

"I was fairly certain that I was your muse." A smug smirk tweaked the hair of his neatly trimmed beard as he slowly spun her desk chair around to face him. Leaning in, he propped himself up on the arms of the chair to cage her in.

Mari tilted her chin up with a slow grin and breathed him in deeply. Now only steps from the beach, his masculine and woodsy scent had intermingled enticingly with the sea air. His wardrobe choices had finally improved with her help. The collared shirt was rolled up to his elbows. It displayed his now lightly tanned and muscular forearms. He always left the first few buttons undone. Mari enjoyed that little tease of the dip of his collarbone and chest hair.

"You are. And…" Her fingers were already working their way through the buttons of his shirt as she leaned up to press a suckling kiss against his neck. A warm sigh of delight answered her back. "I think I need a refill on your muse powers…"

Ben offered her a rakish grin as her fingers glided along his bare skin between the parted sides of his shirt. In one swift movement, he scooped her up in her arms. Mari let out a surprised squeal that turned into a bubble of giggles. With a heated kiss, he headed to the bedroom to offer the author her requested *inspiration*.

Bonus Epilogue

One year after they first laid eyes on each other through the bakery case…

The warm enchantment of the sun's rays through the curtains eased Mari from the comforts of sleep. Rolling onto her back, she stretched with a soft yawn. As her hands dropped back to the bed, she realized the bed next to her was empty. It wasn't exactly a surprise. She had spent the better part of the previous evening writing again and it was well into the late morning.

Shifting beneath the sheets, she smiled as she rolled over onto her side. The chill of the empty bedding in the air conditioning teased her naked skin as her mind drifted back to when she had settled into bed. Ben had been sound asleep but the gentle jostling of her slipping between the sheets had roused him. He didn't like to disturb her when she was in the writing zone, but once she was free, he typically pounced. Despite such a late hour, his hungry hands sought her out in the darkness.

It was difficult to believe that a year ago both of them were a bumbling embarrassment to the dating world. Now here they were, living together, in their beloved shore town, as they waited out the building of the beach house of their dreams. Mari's book, *Romancing the Pages*, had been wildly successful. She was in talks to get it turned into a movie. It was a whole new process but one that she was beyond excited about.

Wonderful Ben had been a welcomed steadfast rock in her life. He offered constant support and encouragement with each new project she took on. The words continued to flow as easily as a year ago. Faith was been thrilled, along with Mari's publisher. There was no stopping her now.

Ben had roused early for work, but not without giving Mari a tender kiss. In her sleepiness she barely registered the notion, it felt more like a dream. Flopping over, she slowly sat herself up, only to have her wildly tousled hair tumble down over her eyes. With a grin, she took her hand and shoved her hair back. She went to get out of bed but something on the nightstand caught her eye.

A single red rose accompanied a white envelope with Mari's name elegantly scrawled on it. She wondered when Ben had a moment to find such an elegant specimen of a flower. Plucking the card from the nightstand, she ripped it open. On a white index card was a note:

Happy 1st Anniversary, Darling.
One year ago today I first laid eyes on you through the case in the bakery.
You haven't left my thoughts since that moment.
Speaking of the bakery, there's a sweet treat waiting for you there from me.

See you later for our dinner date.

Love, Ben

She let out a sweet little croon as she held the note to her chest for a moment. She hadn't exactly taken careful note of the first day that she met Ben. But here he was, keeping track of it all along. Picking up the rose, she brought it to her nose as she wandered into the bathroom to get ready for the day.

* * *

"Hey, girl!" Shannon called out with the biggest grin as she watched Mari enter Kohler's Bakery. She almost seemed to be bursting at the seams as she quickly shuffled her way around the counter to embrace her friend. "Shit, oh my god, I've got you covered in powdered sugar! My bad."

She laughed and brushed off the white dust easily. "Good morning to you too." Glancing up, she craned her neck around the quiet bakery, looking for Ben's alluded surprise. "Did…Ben leave something here for me?"

"Oh!" Shannon exclaimed with a clap of her hands and an excited bounce. "He sure did!" Disappearing behind the counter, she popped up with a brown bag and another envelope. "He also ordered you a cup of coffee, just give me a second." Handing the things across the counter to Mari, she turned and quickly went about making up the coffee order.

"What's this?" Mari asked in question as she rotated the envelope with curiosity. It had her name in Ben's elegant hand, much like the other envelope from earlier that morning.

Shannon shrugged, not meeting her gaze. "No idea. He came in this morning and grabbed his breakfast before ordering yours." Peeking into her bag, Mari grinned at the sight of two cream-filled donuts inside. Pulling one out, she devoured it as Shannon put the finishing touches on the coffee. Shannon placed her cup on the counter with an odd smile. "Don't be a stranger. Come up for air sometimes with your writing binges." Shannon teased and Mari nodded her acknowledgement with a laugh as she left the bakery.

Taking a few steps down the street towards her car, Mari suddenly remembered the odd envelope from Ben. Tearing it open there was yet another note. This time it was a bit more cryptic:

I hope you enjoyed breakfast.
Assuming you slept in, it's probably close to the lunch hour.
Head to the Wind Drift for a drink on me.

Love, Ben

With a ripe blush on her cheeks, she let out a huff of laughter. The Wind Drift had technically been their first official/unofficial date. She had drunk so much alcohol that night that she had barely touched it since. But if it hadn't been for that embarrassing night, she wouldn't be where she was today.

On the drive over, she ate the remaining donut and finished off her coffee. At least now she was sufficiently fed for a dose of alcohol. Stepping up to the bar, the bartender smiled at her before procuring a bottle of her favorite hard cider and yet another card. Looking at him in question, she nodded her thanks and tore open the card as she plopped down on a stool.

Even though you almost took my head off with a golf ball, our mini-golf date will always be memorable. Relive all our awkwardness with a round.
Just mention your name. They'll know what to do.

Love, Ben

She outright laughed. What was this odd scavenger hunt game that Ben cooked up? Sipping her cider, she couldn't help but reflect on last summer and all the awkward chaos that ensued. It was the best thing that ever happened to her. With half of her bottle gone, she decided that she needed something a bit healthier than donuts for food. Flagging the bartender, she ordered a summer salad to eat with the rest of the cider.

Following Ben's directions to the letter, Mari headed over to Pirate Island mini golf to play her round of golf. It felt a bit silly to play a round by herself but it was a beautiful day. If she was being honest with herself, she could use a few hours away from writing and have a mental break for the day.

Mari did much better on her round without the handsome distraction of Ben. Walking up to the small hut, she handed over her club only to be given yet another envelope. What was this man up to?

I bet you're a bit overheated from your round of golf. Head over to Sundae Best for some ice cream. Lady's choice.

Love, Ben

He wasn't wrong. Ice cream sounded like a great idea after spending all that time in the afternoon sun. Despite all of these stops prolonging her day, she didn't mind. It was actually rather fun to reminisce about where their relationship had started, compared to what it was now.

Feeling nostalgic, she was happy to see that they had the key lime pie ice cream. For memory's sake, she added on a scoop of gingersnap as well. Although this time, instead of a cone, she opted for a bowl.

As she went to check out, she was handed yet another white envelope. But this time, it had a bit of heft to it.

I know you probably don't have time to run to Wildwood and back, but here are a few quarters to play a game or two and think of me.
Not too much longer until our dinner date!

Love, Ben

Considering that she didn't want to sit in her car and eat ice cream, walking to the nearest arcade along the boardwalk sounded like a much better plan. It was a few blocks down and quite a bit smaller than the arcade at Wildwood. But she knew for sure that they had Skeeball machines. A few rounds would be just the thing.

After four rounds of Skeeball, as she tore off the strip of tickets. It wasn't much but maybe she could at least score a piece of candy or a pencil eraser. Perusing the prize case, she finally made her selection. As the counter attendant handed over her small bounty, she gave Mari yet another envelope. She wracked your brain trying to think where else Ben could send her.

I hope you had fun today.
I enjoyed setting up all these little stops for you to find.

Now come find me at home so I can take you out for our anniversary dinner.

Love, Ben

Grinning, she hurried off to her car. Mari was ready for a shower and some kisses from Ben after he unknowingly teased her all day long. Walking in the door, Ben looked up from his usual reading spot, with his nose in a book. A warm smile greeted her as she scampered over and plopped down into his lap.

"Did you have fun?"

"I did! It was very sweet of you to do that."

Ben smiled and drew her hand up to his lips to place a kiss along her knuckle. "Ready for dinner?"

"I am!" Mari paused thoughtfully. "Let me guess. The same place as our actual first date?"

Ben chuckled with a nod. "You've caught on to my plan." His hands abandoned his book, spread open across his abdomen to keep his page. He looked rather dashing in his dark green button-up shirt and coordinating tie. "I'm ready whenever you are, darling." Brushing a kiss along her jaw, his hands smoothed over her thighs and bottom, draped across his lap. As much as he was hungry for dinner, he was rather famished for something *else*. But all in due time.

"Let me go get a shower and dressed." Leaning in, she cupped his face in her hands and brought his mouth to hers. The kiss was slow and sweet before it went a bit sultry. His hands slid up her back, pulling her in closer for a long moment before ushering her off. Mari had a schedule to keep and Ben was doing his best to keep his wits about him.

She shot him a mock pout before sliding off the chair and into the bedroom to get ready. Making sure that she were out of eyesight, Ben reached into his pocket to nervously fumble with a lacquered box. It had been hidden in his drawer for weeks now, just waiting for the right opportunity. He hoped to make it to the first anniversary of *Romancing the Page*'s release, but the excitement and nervousness were eating him alive.

Mari appeared from out of the bedroom almost an hour later, looking ravishing. She had taken the time to curl loose ringlets in her hair that was half pinned back. Her dress was the perfect shade of pink, almost the color of the fluster on her cheeks when Ben really got her going. He took a moment to wonder how he ever ended up so lucky.

Dinner was much different than their previous time at the restaurant. Conversation flowed freely and their body language was in tune with each other's. There were gentle caresses and soft touches along with sweet smiles shared between them both. This time they actually looked like boyfriend and girlfriend. Lovers.

It wasn't until they got in the car to go home that Ben started to get overly nervous. He fumbled with his keys, dropped them twice, and even started to break into a sweat. Mari glanced at him as she sat down in the passenger seat. Concerned, she stroked his temple. He almost jumped clear out of his skin.

"Ben, are you okay? You look a bit...*off*."

"What? Me? N-No...I'm fine." He brushed her off with an odd sort of smile as he started the car. "It's just...I-I remembered I...um...forgot something at the library. Could we swing by on our way home and grab it?"

"Oh, of course," Mari reassured him and he relaxed somewhat. With a nod, he pulled out of the parking spot and headed off down the street to the library. His knuckles were white as he gripped the steering wheel. He had to calm down lest she started thinking something was amiss.

The rehearsal of what he planned to say kept going in his head, almost like a mantra, and it helped even out his demeanor.

"Do you mind coming in with me? It would be helpful to have an extra set of hands to grab stuff."

Mari nodded in acknowledgement but her brow furrowed in question. Just how much did Ben forget at the library? Following him, Ben unlocked the door with some trouble before he held the door for her and turned on the lights. He needed to get a grip, and soon.

"Uh…um…there's a book I need down in non-fiction. D-Do you think you could grab it?" He shakily handed Mari a scrap piece of paper with a Dewey Decimal number on it.

"Ben, there's no title on here." She stated and looked up, but he was already gone. Casting a quick glance around and not seeing any sign of him, she shrugged.

"You'll know it when you see it!" His voice sounded like it came from his office and Mari chuckled with a nod. Looking back at the number, she set off down the aisles of books towards the non-fiction section. Ironically enough it was down the aisle next to her old preferred table in the library. The one that she had spent most of her days last summer writing at.

Shuffling down the aisle, her eyes scanned the book spines in her search. You were getting closer and closer… And then, she saw it.

It was a black leather-bound book that looked out of place among the plastic-protected books on the shelf. But what stood out the most was the most elegant gold leaf lettering that said "To My Love" along the spine.

Curious, she plucked it from the shelf and opened it to the first page. What she found amongst the pages was a beyond beautiful handmade leather journal that was full of every single sweet thought that Ben had of Mari.

Tears immediately sprung to her eyes as she slowly flipped through the pages. It spanned their entire summer of awkward nonsense with dated journal entries intermittent with random thoughts or ideas. There were even a few of their game tickets and other random memorabilia inside, lovingly taped to the corresponding pages. It must have taken him weeks to write this all out in such a sweet keepsake.

There were a bunch of blank pages in the back for more to be filled in. When she arrived at the last written journal page, all it had was today's date and the words:

Today I asked if

Mari looked up to go off in search of Ben in question but instead found him at the end of the aisle of books.

Down on one knee.

She felt her heart stall as he timidly held up a small lacquered wooden ring box and opened it. Inside was a stunning solitaire diamond ring.

"Today I asked if you would marry me." His words were firm and true, with no hint of any nervous waver. He knew that he wanted to spend the rest of his life with her.

"Ben…" There was a warble to her voice as she closed the gap between them. Tears formed in her eyes. As soon as she was within reach, his free hand reached out to grasp hers. Nodding in disbelief, her acknowledgment tumbled out in an increasingly louder jumble of words. "Yes! Oh my god, yes!"

A bright grin split his face and he released the breath that he had been holding as he awaited her answer. Relief washed over him before excitement took over. Tears made his ocean-blue eyes glisten in the fluorescent light of the library. Inelegantly fumbling with the ring, he managed to slip it from the box and lovingly slide it onto her awaiting ring finger.

    Biting her bottom lip, Mari let out a surprised huff of joy before flinging herself at Ben. Wrapping her arms around him, she pulled him down hard to her mouth for a long kiss. Ben laughed when he managed to break free, pressing his forehead against hers with a grin.

About the Author

K. Iwancio has been an interior designer, graphic designer, artist, teacher, volunteer, and now an independently published author. She has visited far-off planets, been on movie sets, and even checked some things off her Bucket List. One of her secret talents is her vast knowledge of Star Wars trivia. She lives in South Central Pennsylvania.

www.kiwancio.com

Made in United States
Troutdale, OR
06/29/2024